To those who were there
and to those who remain.

ANOTHER MAN'S *Life*

A Novel

By Steven W. Horn

GPP GRANITE
PEAK PRESS Cheyenne
Cheyenne, Wyoming
www.granitepeakpress.com

GPP GRANITE PEAK PRESS Cheyenne

Granite Peak Press
www.granitepeakpress.com

This book is a work of fiction. All references to real people, actual events, and places must be read as fiction. The characters in this book are creations of the author's imagination, as is the town of Keotonka, Iowa. The dialogue is invented.

First printing 2012

ISBN: 978-0-9835894-2-6

LCCN: 2011940186

Acknowledgments

With thanks to Jim Wangberg, Tonya Talbert, Michael and Kathleen O'Neal Gear, and Peter Decker who read and offered encouragement, as well as friendship.

I am indebted to Sue Collier for her expertise in the many aspects of book publishing.

Special thanks to my daughters, Tiffany, Melissa, and Amanda, whose edits were helpful and whose support was unfailing. This book exists because of the loving support and fierce advocacy of my wife, Margaret, who has never stopped believing in me.

CHAPTER 1

"He wondered if he ought to write a swan-song,
but laughed the thought away. There was no time.
He was impatient to be gone."
Jack London
Martin Eden

5:15 a.m.

HE WOULD LET HER SLEEP FOR ANOTHER HOUR. The day ahead would be hard on her. He would go to the barn. Eden wanted things to be simple for her.

He picked up the letter. The Great Seal of the United States embossed in gold gave the letterhead its intended authority. The blindfolded lady holding the balance in front of her intimidated him. He knew there would be no balance, no justice. Her scales would be tipped decidedly toward meaningless partisan, political objectives. The United States Department of Justice had convened a grand jury. The Senate hearings had given the president and attorney general little choice.

*****

Outside, the August corn flagged gently in the predawn Iowa breeze. Soon the fields would gain color as the sun crept above the wooded hills to the east. Already the peak of the barn and silvery dome of the silo were reflecting the first blush of day. When the sun reached the top of the barn door he would go.

Inside, the advancing light brought definition to the room. Every surface presented a memory of a life lived. Fifty-seven years of a man's life represented by an odd collection of mementos: a pinecone from Scotland, an oak fern stand that was her grandmother's, Buddy's leather collar and tags. The room was comfortable. Photographs told the story, the epic that preceded him. Not the entire story, but the parts that should be preserved. Immigrants in ill-fitting clothes, babies in white christening gowns, graduations, hopeful couples—all represented by less than a second of their lives captured on film. Most were of Elizabeth's side of the family. He had wanted it that way. It was her ancestral home and land. He was an outsider, a stranger passing by who had stopped to work for room and board. There were gaps in his story, dead spots that haunted him every day: holes that would soon be filled.

Jessica's life visually unfolded from every available surface within the room. As their only child she did not have to compete for shelf space. The preteen years were the most photographed. By the age of fifteen her childlike cuteness had been replaced with the rebelliousness of a teenager. She'd quickly outgrown the defiant years and then she had been gone. She was thirty-four now.

Her life with him seemed so long ago, a patchwork of recollections captured as still life. But he could animate each photo. He could feel his lungs burn as he ran beside her bicycle, training wheels removed. He felt the heat of an Iowa July and the stickiness of sweat on his arms as he officiated the watermelon eating contest that she won. He could hear the crunch of dry leaves and smell the crispness of fall as he led her to the pumpkin patch down by the river where she always selected the most misshapen pumpkin for her Jack-o'-lantern. Unbeknownst to anyone, he still planted that lower corner of the field to pumpkins every year and then plowed them under in November. He loved his daughter as if she were his own.

Remembrances, the past reinvented, he thought as he slowly scanned the room. His life seemed an odd collection of memories, a collage of colorless images without order, separated by the unmemorable routine of making a living. Some had dimension, vivid reminders of what he wanted to forget, the ones that took his breath away. They were the ones he could not share with Elizabeth. They were the ones that the rest of the world now wanted.

Looking at the letter again, he read, "Dear Mr. Cain: You are hereby summoned to appear—" He inhaled slowly, his chest rising. He held his breath. Through flared nostrils he exhaled with finality. He felt strangely relieved. It had been a long time. There would be no resolution, no absolution, only a millisecond of peace. He placed the letter on the end table next to the revolver.

CHAPTER 2

"No civilised troops in the world could have endured the hell through which they came. Their business was to destroy what lay in front of them."
Rudyard Kipling
The Light That Failed

1971

"INCOMING! WE'VE GOT INCOMING! Rat Man's dead! Jesus Christ! Get some air!" Eden yelled, his flight helmet visor awash in blood.

"Roger that, Cowboy," Lonnie said as the Huey began to climb. "Did you get a fix?"

"I can't see shit over here." The glare of the morning sun on his side of the helicopter made the jungle beneath him appear silvery and without detail. The brass shell casings in the bandoleer feeding his M-60 reflected painfully into his eyes. "Looks like we took it from the port side. Little Nail, what the hell? Over."

"Smoke," Brad 'Little Nail' Holcomb yelled from the port gun bay. "We've got smoke at eight o'clock. Confirm."

"Yeah, we've got it," Lonnie said. The chopper pitched sharply to the left and downward. "Anything that looks like a possible LZ?"

There was silence as the four remaining crew members looked for an opening, a landing zone, in the jungle canopy. Rat Man, the radio operator, was slumped forward against his harness, his head uncomfortably turned sideways against the radio console. His face, with unflinching eyes, was turned toward Eden's gun bay. His neck from just below the jaw line to his collar bone was gone.

There was a marshy area in the oxbow of a small river, but it was at least a half mile from the plume of white smoke drifting upward from a small clearing to the east. Muzzle flashes appeared along a perimeter on both the northern and eastern flanks of the ground recon team who had tossed the smoke canisters.

"Too tight," John "Gaseous" Clay reported from the copilot seat. "We'll slice and dice if we try to set it down in there."

"Cowboy, you juice 'em when we come in," Lonnie ordered Eden. "Little Nail, you drop the strings," he said, referring to the McQuire rigs, a swing-like seat attached to a rope lowered through the trees.

"RT Yellowstone, this is Pony Boy come to save your ass. Over."

"This is RT Yellowstone's One-Two. It's about time a Pony showed up. They're all over us. No way we'll make the river. Where's your support? Over."

"You're looking at the extent of U.S. military involvement over Laos. How many are you? Over."

"We be six."

"We can take four. You decide. Any Yards?"

There was a short delay. "Pony Boy, this is the RT's One-One. You'll have to make two extractions. We will not leave our Yards. I repeat: We will not leave our Yards. Over."

Lonnie could hear the full auto bursts of rifle fire through his headset. He knew how protective the ground teams became of their Montagnard trackers.

"We copy, One-One. Four strings are all we have. Double up if you can. No guarantees on a second extraction unless we get air support and we'd be calling them in right on top of you. Charlie is knocking on your door at less than a click. Over."

"Hurry, for Christ's sake. Out."

"Show 'em what you got, Cowboy," Lonnie said as the chopper came out of a steep bank and broadsided the east flank of North Vietnamese Army regulars who rushed angrily toward the trapped recon team.

Immediately, the muzzle flashes from below were followed by the stinging slap of bullets slamming into the armor plating of the chopper's hull. Eden began spraying the jungle in a wide arc where he had seen the advancing line of NVA. The tracer rounds drew straight lines in the air. Hot, empty casings filled the bay at the end of his right swing. He did not aim at individuals. He wanted to slow their advance, pin them down, buy some time.

The Huey banked to a halt over the break in the trees. Lonnie pivoted the craft violently to port, allowing Eden to strafe the charging line from the north, then back to starboard. Brad tossed the strings, two from the port door and two from the starboard. Gaseous, leaning against the door, guided Lonnie by calling out the meters from the McQuire harness to the ground.

"Little Nail, give 'em some support on the north," Lonnie ordered.

Brad crawled back into his gun bay and began firing, his barrel pointing acutely downward.

"Touchdown. Steady," Gaseous said calmly.

"Pony Boy, this is Bird Dog. Do you copy? Over."

"We copy, Bird Dog. Where you be? Over."

"We be on the top, you be on the bottom. As it should be. Over."

Lonnie twisted his head upward to see the little Cessna 0-1 Bird Dog high above them. "I need a minute, Bird Dog. We've got six on the ground, four strings, and we're taking heavy fire. Over."

"Pony Boy, this is Covey Rider. Over."

"Oh shit," Lonnie said before pressing his mike button. He knew that a Covey Rider in the right seat of a Forward Air Controller meant an air strike was imminent. "Go ahead, Covey Rider. Over."

"Pony Boy, a covey is on the way with an ETA of forty-five seconds. I won't wave them off. Make it good, make it fast. Over."

"Where we at, Gaseous?" Lonnie said.

"Steady this son of a bitch. They can't catch the strings. It's a firefight down there."

Brad and Eden shifted frantically in their seats, a blur of casings ejecting from their guns. Both lines of NVA had pressed forward to within fifty yards of the recon team. The Huey hovered just above the tree line. AK-47 rounds riddled the hull and ricocheted noisily between the gun bays. Seventy-five feet below, the recon team repeatedly attempted to reach the strings that danced temptingly in the small clearing. Each time, enemy fire drove them back into the bush.

"Cowboy, pop red smoke," Lonnie said.

"Jesus Christ, Lonnie. Give 'em one more shot at it," Eden said, his voice pleading. He swung the M-60 quickly to his left and cut down four NVA who had boldly rushed into the clearing.

"Lay it down now!" Lonnie ordered. "We're out of time."

Eden stopped firing and yanked a smoke canister from the door support. He pulled the pin and, leaning half out the bay, heaved the canister past the clearing toward the enemy.

"One away. Let me put another one down for some cover," Eden said.

He tossed the second canister toward the other flank of oncoming NVA. His arm tingled and the fingers of his left hand felt stiff. He began firing. But he fired alone.

"Little Nail!" Eden yelled into the mike. There was no response. Looking to the cockpit, he saw Gaseous twisting in his seat attempting to look into Brad's gun bay.

"Ten seconds, Lonnie. Give 'em ten seconds for Christ's sake," Eden said.

The dense red smoke engulfed the clearing. Eden could no longer see what he was shooting at, but he continued to lay down fire. The McGuire rigs disappeared into the red fog below.

"Pony Boy, this is Covey Rider. You have fifteen seconds. You'll need half of them to clear the zone. Over."

"We're counting, Covey Rider. Out." Lonnie turned toward Clay. "Tight-assed son of a bitch. You see anything, Gaseous?"

Gaseous had his head pressed against the bubble and stared downward. He did not respond. Lonnie reached over and grabbed his shoulder. "Gaseous?"

John Clay fell backward, his head bobbing against his chest. The hole in his visor was the same size as the one in the Plexiglas window below him. "Oh, sweet mother of Jesus!" Lonnie cried.

"Ten seconds, Pony Boy."

The helicopter rose vertically, slowly at first, then quickly when Lonnie guessed the strings had cleared the jungle canopy. Violently, he banked to port and accelerated toward the river.

"Cowboy, what'd we catch?" Lonnie asked.

Eden strained against his harness to see below the acutely banked craft. Three men on two strings were clinging for their lives to the ropes that trailed almost horizontally from the steeply banked Huey.

"Three with one double," Eden said. "We'll lose the one if we don't sit down soon."

"We're headed for the oxbow."

Shadows swept over the helicopter, followed by a shrill roar that drowned out the sound of the rotor. Eden looked up to see the bellies of three F-4 Phantoms. They were so close that he could see the red nose cones on the 500-pound bombs strapped beneath their wings as they honed in on the red smoke.

The jungle in and around the smoke opened widely to expose the dark earth below its roots. Giant craters appeared and within a second were filled with an inward-rolling, orange flame. The fireball was surrounded by a dark circle of jungle expulsion; planetary fragments catapulted skyward.

A pair of F-100 Super Sabers followed, their cannons riddling the smoke-filled Laotian forest ahead of them. They dropped cluster bombs as they passed. Trees appeared to recede as they dropped on their stumps before gracefully falling over.

Eden fought the lump in his throat and ignored the wet, throbbing pain in his arm as the propeller-driven A-1 Skyraiders lumbered by, their South Vietnamese insignia proudly displayed. He watched in horror as the horizon ignited in a rolling log of orange flames from the napalm they released. The sterilization was complete. All traces removed. There would be no evidence and no embarrassment to a president who convincingly lied to America that they were not in Laos.

CHAPTER 3

"A second convention was that we had no cruel or ambitious or ignorant commanders. . . . disorganized insanity . . . was not only foreseen but a part of a grander strategy out of which victory would emerge."
John Steinbeck
Once There Was a War

1971

THE SMELL OF ALCOHOL WAS SO STRONG THAT EDEN'S nostrils flared with defiance. The antiseptic smell competed with, but did not displace, the stench of urine and body odor that filled the makeshift hospital. The commotion was deafening. The Vietnamese language, a confusing garble of human noises uttered in fast-forward, filled the elongated Quonset. Dozens of refugees clamored for attention in the half-round corridor. There were no rooms. Faded signs written in French declared administrative and medical functions. Gurneys lined the curved walls. Bandaged GIs, many with their jungle boots sticking out from under blood soaked sheets, lay atop the wheeled carts. Plastic tubing from suspended IV bags gracefully enjoined the arms of both the conscious and unconscious. Bags of urine and large glass carboy jugs with drain tubes stuffed in their necks sat below the gurneys. The civilians, tiny and dark, lay curled on grass mats on the floor. Their relatives wailed above them.

Eden sat in an aqua-colored, contoured plastic chair with tapered metal legs that ended with pod-like feet. A scowling, elderly Vietnamese woman yelled with nonstop, staccato gibberish into his face. Her gold teeth sparkled amid red gums, stained from the betel-nut root she had chewed most of her life. Her breath reeked of nouc mam and cheroots, a lethal combination of rotting fish and burned rubber that made Eden light-headed. He had no idea what she wanted. His bandaged left arm burned and throbbed.

"*Di di,*" Eden said. "*Di di mau.*" He waved his right hand at her in a motion for her to go away. She ignored him.

"Go on. Git, you shriveled up old bag of shit," someone said. A large olive drab figure suddenly appeared in front of Eden. The old woman was hip checked and sent to all fours among the mass of human squalor on the floor.

"Eden, you ole cowboy," Ivan said, a wide smile across his face.

Eden looked up, puzzled. "What are you doing here, Goose?"

"Come to decorate you, shit for brains." He thrust a small paper box at Eden.

"What's this?"

"It's your Purple Heart. You can open it later. Let's get out of here. This place stinks."

"How'd this happen? Who put me in for it? I just got here," Eden said.

"Lonnie Webster, your pilot. I just pushed it around eight or ten assholes, got the general to sign the papers, and thought I would deliver it myself," Ivan said. He grinned broadly down at Eden.

"What did she want?" Eden asked, nodding in the direction of the mamasan who was struggling to her feet.

"Oh, she was just telling you how much she appreciated American intervention in Southeast Asia. How much better off she is since we arrived. How most of her family has gone on to better lives as insects and lizards and those that remain really didn't mind sacrificing their legs and arms. And something about a 10 percent discount if we visit her fifteen-year-old granddaughter who's a whore in Da Nang."

"Christ, Goose. I'm glad to see you're as sardonic as always," Eden said.

"Sardonic? That's a pretty big word for a shot-up, dumb shit door gunner," Ivan said.

Eden smiled as they made their way from the evac hospital. He tossed his paperwork into an overflowing trash can by the door. Ivan had been his friend since they had met in boot camp at Fort Lewis. Awkwardly tall and spindly with a cartoon-like Adam's apple, the drill sergeant had told him he looked like a goose. The name stuck. Exceptionally high test scores had landed him a job as an aide to the commanding general of the XXIV Corps.

"Where we going?"

"I borrowed the General's car and driver," Ivan said, pointing to the shiny, black Fairlane 500 with a red three-star flag on the front fender. "We're going to the USO Club at China Beach. Mamie Van Doren is singing. I saw her in Saigon. She acts like Marilyn Monroe with a brain injury. She dry humps guys from the audience and pretty much gives herself an orgasm with the microphone cord. You'll love it."

*****

Somewhere near Marble Mountain, Eden began to cry.

Ivan said nothing. Instead, he squeezed the back of Eden's neck and, without warning, punched his bandaged arm. "Let me give you something to cry about," he said.

Eden took a deep breath, held it, and looked out the side window. Wiping the tears from his eyes, he continued to look away from Ivan. "Five of us left Da Nang less than ten hours ago," he said. "Two of us came back." He took another deep breath in an attempt to stop the tears. "We picked up three so I guess it was a wash. No, wait a second. We fried three of ours on the ground. So, of the eleven of us who were in Laos this morning, five are alive. Shit, we're down six. Not fair. Whose turn is it?" he said turning to look at Ivan.

"It's their turn, Cowboy," Ivan said. "It's always their turn."

*****

Illumination flares drifted slowly downward, their tiny parachutes caught in the evening breeze above the river. The outline of guard towers, sandbag bunkers, and concertina wire defined the perimeter of XXIV Corps Headquarters. Ivan had insisted that Eden stay with him that evening. They sat on the sandbag wall outside Ivan's hooch, drinking warm Budweiser and smoking Salems.

"You've got to admit, she had great tits," Ivan said suddenly, referring to Mamie Van Doren.

Eden continued to stare at the river. Just the ripples reflected the light of the flares. Half a dozen beers had not cheered him up. "What are we doing here, Goose?"

"Just putting in our time; it's kind of like olive drab welfare. It's a great way to get guys off the streets and put them to work for the good of the country. With good behavior, I'm out in four months."

"No. I mean America. What's the U.S. doing here?"

"You mean besides stomping out oppression and deterring the advancement of communist aggression?"

Eden frowned and shook his head. "This war is on political hold. It's in a maintenance mode. We're just going through the fucking motions with no intentions of winning. Christ."

Ivan knew that Eden was in no mood for his humorous remarks. He drank from his beer can and looked out over the river.

"Nixon is a goddamn liar," Eden said.

"No shit."

"He's got the public convinced that we're not in Cambodia or Laos. Where the hell do you think I was this morning? The only offensive we've got going in this war is on the other side of the borders. We're bombing the crap out of them in Laos. There are sorties leaving Da Nang and Udorn every hour around the clock. It seems like one of those flyboys goes down every other day. Then they send those gung ho mothers, SOG, into the bush to extract their asses. Who are those crazy bastards, anyway? Then we get to go in to pull the whole lot of them out. But not until they've got Charlie whipped into a frenzy." Eden took another drink of beer. "You know how many pilots we've recovered in the last nine months?"

Ivan did not respond. He knew the answer.

"None," Eden said. "Not a fucking one." He lit a cigarette and coughed. "You know, I only smoke when I drink. Or is it I only drink when I smoke? It doesn't matter." He paused then looked squarely at Ivan. "I think our job is to groundtruth their location, to pinpoint their sorry little asses so the scorched earth brigade can toast them. I don't even think those SOG recon teams are there to recover pilots. Why the hell would they be carrying twenty-two caliber pistols with silencers? The damn few we've pulled out are loaded down with recovered Viet Cong documents. Shit, Goose, they're on intelligence runs. They're not looking for flyboys. The dummies don't realize they're no better off than the pilots. We'll tenderize and barbecue them too, if it looks like they're going to get caught."

"Look, my friend," Ivan said. "You and I can talk about such things because we're both Special Operations Group cleared. We've been through the drill. I've got the highest security clearances known to man. There isn't anything they don't know about me or my family. If you even hint of this to anyone else, they'll never find your sorry ass. More than likely, they'll cover up your carcass with mine. So be cool, man. Put it out of your head. Just do your job and get stateside."

"I thought SOG stood for Studies and Observations Group," Eden said.

Ivan chuckled. "That's its new name. It sounds less Special Forces and more rear academics. You best forget about them both."

"How do we know where to find the pilots?" Eden asked, ignoring the warning. "Sometimes they are miles from the crash site. Depends on where they bail out, I guess. But how do we get their coordinates?"

"They have radios."

"That's bull and you know it," Eden said. "Even if they were using their radios deep in enemy territory, we still couldn't get that exact of a fix. We fly right to them. If they are on the move when we get our orders, Da Nang calls and gives us the new coordinates sometimes within minutes of our arrival. We're tracking them, aren't we?"

"The bomber crews all have transponders sewn into their flight suits," Ivan said. He turned away and followed a flare that drifted lazily toward the river.

"Do they know about it?"

"Eden," Ivan said, with a strong note of seriousness in his voice. "You're my friend. You need to be cool about all this. This shit will get you in big trouble. It'll get us both in big trouble."

"Do they know about it?" Eden repeated.

Ivan stared at him for a long moment. "No."

"Are the transponders there so they can be rescued?" Eden asked.

"In theory. If it's a cake walk, we'll snatch 'em up." Ivan paused. "But you said it yourself, our success rate sucks."

"Depends on where they go down," Eden said. "If it's across the border, there's no slack. The covey suddenly appears and we're ordered to withdraw." He took a long drag on his Salem, lifted his head skyward, and blew the smoke in a long plume into the warm, tropical night. "Our job is to confirm them, pop smoke, and get out of Dodge. Isn't it?" Tears were forming in his eyes again. "They have no intention of rescue. Do they?" Eden took a deep breath and looked away.

"Come on, Cowboy, give it up. You're getting in way over your head," Ivan said.

"We're whacking the good guys for Christ's sake and I'm an accessory. Don't tell me to give it up. You're not the one doing the killing, you rear echelon motherfucker."

"Neither are you. You're just the guide. The hunters do the killing," Ivan said.

"Three of my friends are dead, Goose. That's the third crew I've had since coming into this country. You want to hear mortality rates? I don't have a chance. I'm going to die trying to kill Americans." Eden looked at his bandaged arm and laughed. "I've been shot twice and neither one of them is worth fifty cents. The million dollar wound just ain't going to happen."

"You never know what's going to happen tomorrow," Ivan said. "We may pull back and stand down. As you said, it's a political war."

Eden inhaled deeply and closed his eyes to stop the tears. The smell of the river was like that of any large river moving slowly into the sea, of mud and fish.

"Who gives the orders?" Eden said.

"For what?"

"Don't fuck with me, Goose."

"It depends. If it's Cambodia, I get a call on the scrambler phone from General McCarthy in Long Binh. He tells me we have a Blue Arrow—a downed pilot—and gives me date, time, and coordinates. It seems like it's always in the middle of the night. They come fetch me when the bells and red lights on the scrambler go off. I wake the Old Man, he dictates a message to the president, sends for a SPECAT from the Command Center."

"What's a SPECAT?"

"A Major with a handcuffed briefcase. The Major gives it to Crypto who sends it EO to Tricky Dicky."

"What are Crypto and EO?" Eden asked, slightly annoyed.

"Crypto is where our cryptographers encrypt—place into code—messages. An EO means Eyes Only. The message is sent TS, SI, EO—Top Secret, Special Intelligence, Eyes Only. The Eyes Only designation means that nobody but the addressee can read it, not even the SPECAT."

"Do you read them?"

"Nope. It's the Old Man, a cryptographer, and the president. But I know what's in them based on the Old Man's response. He reads it and tells me to get the SOG chief. They chew the fat a bit and the Old Man tells me to call McCarthy on the scrambler and inform him that a Bright Light is in progress. A Bright Light is a rescue mission someplace we're not supposed to be."

"What about Laos?" Eden said.

"Same drill only without McCarthy and SOG South. The Old Man handles SOG North. All the incursions from Military Region One start right here."

"I don't get it," Eden said. "Why would we need Nixon's permission to engage in a rescue mission? We're already there, bombing from the air and gathering intelligence on the ground, not to mention all the mercenaries and CIA-types running around. Why the cloak and dagger crap?"

"Those ring-knocking zoomie pilots fresh out of the Academy are the carnival kewpie dolls for Charlie. First prize! They have lots of credibility with the viewing audience. Their mere presence indicates we're bombing. The president has assured the American public and the international community, especially NATO, that we have no military forces in or over Cambodia and Laos. It would be a major loss of face for him if we were discovered."

"So let me get this straight," Eden said, looking directly at Ivan, his eyes squinting. "We're killing American pilots so Nixon won't be caught lying. He authorizes each of their murders?"

"You know these airborne, gung ho, green-machine types. They have a code of honor that says they will leave no man behind, even their dead. We've lost a lot of men in this war trying to recover dead guys. Shit." Ivan shook his head and spit, "At the same time, they'll blindly execute an order even if it means eating their young. The commanding generals won't order a tactical air strike on their own men, but they'll carry out an order, especially if it comes from the commander in chief."

"A Bright Light really isn't a rescue mission?"

"Yes and no. When you get your orders, we give you a head start. We know your ETA. We then scramble air command for a strike at the same location. If you can snatch them quickly, they're home free and the strike is waved off."

"It hasn't worked yet," Eden said. "Not a single goddamned pilot; only a handful of those crazy bastards from

SOG." He flipped his cigarette butt toward the swirl of wire at the perimeter fence. "Does MACV know what the hell is going on here?"

"Not really. Damn it, Cowboy. Enough."

"What about the Joint Chiefs?"

"No."

"You mean to tell me—"

"I didn't mean to tell you anything," Ivan said, sharpness in his voice. "You need to stop asking so damn many questions. You know a hundred times more than any other stupid door gunner. You keep your pie hole shut and watch your back."

Eden ignored him. "I read in *Stars and Stripes* sometime back that Congress had passed a law saying we couldn't go into Laos."

"That was the Cooper-Church Amendment. They were so pissed off when they found out about what we were doing in Cambodia, they thought they'd shut Tricky Dicky out of Laos. Ha! That's why they call him Tricky. The son of a bitch has his own secret little war going on."

"Why? What's in it for him?" Eden asked.

"Man, you have no idea how close we are to losing this war. Nixon wants to kick ass and save face, but those bleeding hearts in Congress keep tying his hands. We'd of lost it by now except we've been so disruptive to Charlie's build-ups in Laos. You mark my words, Cowboy, they'll spill in from Laos and take Hue, Quang Tri, Da Nang, and the rest of Region One. As soon as they recover in Cambodia, they'll do the same to Saigon. It's only a matter of time."

"Then why don't we just go home and let the greasy little gooks have it?"

"What? And screw up Tricky Dicky's reelection plans? I don't think so. He hates Democrats more than Commies. The

Dems in Congress have done everything they can to prolong this war and make Nixon look bad. The last thing they want is for him to win reelection next year."

Eden looked at him with disbelief. "When do you make all this shit up?"

"Grow up, Cowboy. This war has nothing to do with truth, justice, and the American way. It's about four more years of Nixon. Like a comedy routine, timing is everything. He's trying to keep Charlie from kicking our ass long enough to let Kissinger do his thing in Paris. We'll go home as soon as Henry can negotiate a politically acceptable out to this frigging mess. That, my friend, will occur when Tricky Dicky's political strategists tell him it's time."

Ivan lit another cigarette. Exhaling a plume of smoke into the stifling night air, he shook his head. "God, you're naïve. Where'd you go to school, anyway? Bumfuck U? Hey, were there any girls in Wyoming, or just sheep? Can you imagine Mamie Van Doren in a loose-knit wool sweater with no bra?"

A high-pitched ringing in Eden's ears began to drown out Ivan's words. A dull headache at the base of his skull throbbed in unison with the fiery ache in his arm. He wanted to lie down, curl into a ball, and sleep. When he awakened he would be in his own bed at the ranch, Elk Creek, murmuring among the willows, meadowlarks greeting the day.

"What about Mamie Van Doren, caught in a fence, with nothing on but a fleece jacket? You're the herder," Ivan said.

Eden felt too small for his fatigues as he disappeared into the heavy darkness. Grief overwhelmed him.

CHAPTER 4

"From too much love of living,
From hope and fear set free,
We thank with brief thanksgiving
Whatever gods may be
That no life lives forever;
That dead men rise up never;
That even the weariest river
Winds somewhere safe to sea."
Algernon Swinburne
"The Garden of Prosperpine"

5:25 a.m.

HE WOULD SEE THEM PERIODICALLY—MOSTLY AT night, but sometimes during the day when he was tired—their olive drab flight suits moving among the shadows between the rows of corn. They were young and smiling, always silent. They gave Eden the impression of being reluctant participants in some elaborate practical joke. Nearly thirty years had passed, but they were as he remembered them.

He stared at his weak reflection in the glass door of the hall clock. The gold pendulum moved back and forth across his image, rhythmically meting out age. He was not as he remembered. The years were evident in his eyes. Eyes that appeared to have receded from a world he no longer wanted to see. In their wake were the creases of time, sharp angles that radiated outward, furrows created from the skeptical explosion within his eyes. Eyes that had seen too much. He righted the wedding ring on his swollen finger. Aging was exposed in the morning, he thought. Graceful, perhaps, but parts of him ached, some hurt. But he was alive.

Mark Rottman, Brad Holcomb, John Clay, and a score of others appeared as he remembered them. Not as bloody, mangled corpses, but smiling young men with no future. He always saw them as being happy. He could see Brad's eyes shine and his twisted smile when he moved cleverly on the chessboard.

Since he had never tried to contact the men who had survived with him, they appeared as they had been, too. All except LaFollette, who had appeared five months earlier on a national news broadcast, his shifty eyes darting nervously on either side of his hawk nose. He had repeatedly pushed his long, greasy hair away from his pocked face in order to stuff a cigarette between his quivering lips. The crazy Cajun was reported as a homeless veteran who lived on the streets of D.C. Yet, he had managed to help trigger a Congressional inquiry, the appointment of a special prosecutor, and the seating of a grand jury. Pretty impressive, Eden thought, for a junkie door gunner who lived on a steam grate and sold MIA/POW bracelets at the Wall. But, the media had fueled the fire. Not since Watergate had they been so voracious. They smelled blood on the Republicans and the feeding frenzy that followed gave Congressional Democrats the courage to overreact.

Nixon was dead. Eden had smiled with relief when he had heard the news. He remembered how dumbfounded Elizabeth had been by his lighthearted behavior when he'd learned of the former president's death. The man he had once regarded as the Great Satan was dead. For so many years, Nixon had been the Antichrist in Eden's mind, an evildoer of irrational proportion who deserved something worse than death. With time, he questioned his indictment of Nixon. He knew that his hatred for the man had taken on mythical qualities in the early years. But it was easy to assign blame to a fallen president. The pain Eden felt, the guilt that would claim him when the sun reached the barn door, the shame of an entire generation were all easily placed at Nixon's feet. There was a time when he would have watched with amusement had Congress wanted to drag Nixon's rotting corpse through the streets of the nation's capital for all to see. But now they wanted Eden to ride the horse that would do the dragging. He would have no part of it. Either way, Elizabeth and Jessica would soon figure it out. LaFollette would implicate him.

He picked up the letter again and stared at it without reading. How could such an insignificant person like himself be needed to rewrite history? What about the big brass? Was Abrams dead? What about Weyand or even Westmoreland? Ellsworth Bunker was an old ambassador thirty years ago. If any of them were still alive, they were probably eating soft food and being changed twice a day. He had heard that even the Joint Chiefs did not know. But the brass at XXIV Corps knew. It had all been very confusing for a twenty-four-year-old. He was unable to figure out who the players were and what roles they played. Nothing was as it seemed. No one would have believed that an American president, eight thousand miles away, was directing part of the war effort without the knowledge of the Big Green Machine, the Armed Forces themselves.

Then there was the CIA, who seemed to be everywhere. He had learned there was no such thing as an American civilian in Southeast Asia. Corporate America was a front for the CIA in 'Nam. Shell, Philco, Singer, Air America were all players in the intelligence game. He had flown as many civilians into and out of Cambodia and Laos as military. It was often impossible to tell who the military were. SOG uniforms had no identification of any type. Even their weaponry was unconventional. Stubby CAR-15 submachine guns with their folding wire stocks, sometimes 9mm Swedish K's, sawed-off shotguns, mini-grenade launchers, and High Standard 22 pistols with silencers. Mercenary forces were an amalgam of nondescript assassins. From Vietnamese Montagnards, Laotian Hmongs, and Korean Marines to renegade American deserters, the common thread appeared to be the CIA. Suntanned American businessmen in tan suits and straw hats sometimes rode with them and calmly called in tactical air strikes north of the DMZ.

*****

Rodney the Rhode Island Red rooster crowed in his offbeat fashion from a perch somewhere in the barnyard. He noted that the sun had moved below the mow door of the barn. A feed bunk door clanged noisily from the pigpen. The sky was cloudless. It would be another hot day. He placed the letter back on the table and quietly rose from the chair.

From the locked gun case in the den he retrieved the green tin box. He opened the miniature padlock with a safety pin and sat down at his desk. Beth and Jessica had never seen the contents of the box. Once, when asked, he had told his wife it contained ammunition. It was his secret. It held an odd assortment of mementos that represented a mere two year period of his life, a period of time that existed only for him. No one ever questioned it and if they did, he quickly changed the subject. For a decade after the war, nobody bothered to ask. People did not want to know. Then a new generation became curious about, almost fascinated by, America's involvement in Vietnam. They seemed to forget the loss and forgive the mistake. But he would never forget and forgive, especially Nixon.

There had been a renewed sense of patriotism that swept across the country in the months following the September attacks on New York and the Pentagon. But, as the War on Terrorism dragged on, a receding economy and accusations of political mismanagement replaced the sense of nationalism with apathy and skepticism. The Republicans were scrambling for new leadership, with Senator Winston Tucker the easy front runner, while the Democrats—led by Senator John Roberts—and the media were rushing to expose the past sins of the Republicans, especially those of Tucker. Eden Cain had been implicated.

He opened the blue, padded leather case with its embossed gold lettering that said "United States of America." The Silver Star hung from its colorful ribbon against the gray, felt interior. Folded into the lid were the accompanying certificate and citation. He read how he had distinguished himself with valor and professionalism against a hostile force in the Republic of Vietnam. The words loyalty, diligence, and devotion were sprinkled liberally within the sentences that proclaimed him to be a credit to himself and the United States Army. There were seven other boxes, each containing different medals, tokens of the government's appreciation for . . . for what, he wondered. For service? For murder? For having the shit shot out of him? He had never shown the medals to anyone. He had not shown Jessica the military scrip that looked like Monopoly money, the blousing rubbers he wore on his pant legs, his dog tags that he wore laced into his jungle boots, or any of the shiny baubles that would have captured the attention of a little girl. Like Elizabeth, his daughter was only vaguely aware that he was a veteran. They knew he had been in the Army, but little more. Early in their relationship, Beth had asked if he had served in Vietnam. He said yes and changed the subject. She never asked again.

Now the entire country would know. But they would learn nothing from Eden Cain.

CHAPTER 5

"The voice of forest water in the night,
a woman's laughter in the dark,
the clean, hard rattle of raked gravel,
the cricketing stitch of midday in hot meadows,
the delicate web of children's voices in the bright air—
these things will never change."
Thomas Wolfe
You Can't Go Home Again

1974

THE SIREN'S SUDDEN WAIL STARTLED HIM. There was no warning, no low pitched prelude. No one else appeared to respond. Keotonka was a town small enough to have a noon siren, a siren that took no leave on weekends or holidays.

Eden's hand shook as he rasped it over two days of whisker stubble below the dark, sleepless hollows of his eyes. He had driven hard across southeastern Wyoming and through the late May heat of Nebraska and Iowa. He had slept briefly in the car the night before on the Iowa side of the Missouri River. A corpulent sheriff's deputy in a crisp, tan uniform had awakened him and searched his '53 Willys Wagon for drugs. Without apology he'd told Eden to move along.

His nose nearly pressed to the window of the town's only café, Eden noted how sparse the lunch crowd was for a Saturday. The town itself was sparse. Main Street stretched east and west for a single block with a good share of its Victorian brick buildings vacant. The Hotel Garfield, a half block to the south, next to the river, seemed unusually large for a one-horse town so removed from the main highway. Les, the grease-streaked attendant at the Texaco station, said the hotel had catered to the river boats that steamed by on their way to Des Moines. "We even had a bawdy house up until World War I," he said, his eyes gleaming with the greatness of the secret divulged. "Logging was king then," he had said. "In the spring they'd float the logs in huge jams all the way to Keokuk."

Les had replaced the thermostat that caused the Willys to limp into town under a plume of steam.

Eden scanned the room, the dark wood booths along the walls and the Formica and chrome tables scattered between. Two guys his age with seed caps, scraggly beards, and big bellies sipped their coffee between animated gestures. An overdressed elderly couple ate in slow motion without speaking. Two teenage girls leaning across the table whispered secrets to each other and giggled. Philodendrons hung in plastic pots from the ceiling; their vines, intertwined, were tied in a spiderweb of straight lines that covered the room. The lone waitress, a thin, middle-aged woman with a pleasant smile and severe hair, stopped in front of the window and motioned for Eden to come in. He pulled back from the window too suddenly. He smiled nervously, looked behind him as if someone had called his name from across the street, then back at the waitress who, again, motioned for him to come in.

A cluster of bells dangling from the top of the door announced his presence. All eyes were suddenly focused on him. There was an uncomfortable silence.

"Hi ya, hon," the waitress called from the middle of the room. "Pay no mind to that sign," she said, nodding at the pedestal near the cash register that stated: Please Wait to Be Seated.

"How 'bout this booth here in the corner?" With menu in hand, she brushed by Eden and led him to the tall booth near the window.

"Don't tell me, I bet you're on your way over to Bentonsport to the bull sale," she said loudly. "Had a number of buyers pass through here in the last two days. Ain't no place to eat over there."

Eden slid into the booth without comment.

"The locals will stop staring at you if they think they know your business," she said softly with a wry smile, placing the menu in front of him.

He looked beyond her. Everyone was still staring.

"What'll it be, dead Angus?" she said loud enough for people in the street to hear. Without waiting for a response, she turned and headed for the kitchen. "I never sold so many patty melts all year as I have in the last couple days. I'll bring you a Pepsi in a minute."

The customers seemed to accept his reason for being there and resumed their lunches. The teenage girls shot glances his way and muffled their giggles with cupped hands.

The waitress brought his Pepsi. She stood there silently and unwrapped his straw.

Eden did not know what to say, but it seemed obvious that she expected him to respond. "I come from a town in Wyoming that's even smaller than Keotonka. If we had a café, people would stare holes in strangers. Thanks for running interference for me."

"You're welcome, hon," she said, smiling. "Just don't stick me for the tab. I'd hate to hunt you down and hurt you." Still smiling, she turned and walked away.

Eden clasped his hands together on top of the table. Since returning from Vietnam, they shook uncontrollably when talking with strangers, especially if anyone asked if he was a veteran. His palms had actually left puddles on the table during his master's defense in Laramie earlier in the spring. The national mood was sour. He quickly learned not to tell people he was a veteran in order to avoid challenging comments or active discrimination. He lived in fear of being discovered. The nation had shamed him.

"Hey good lookin'," a child's voice rang out from across the room followed by giggles of delight.

Eden had not seen a child when scanning the room from the sidewalk. In the far corner of the café, in the booth diagonally opposite from his, he could see the blonde hair of a woman, her back to him. It appeared she was talking to a child beside her in the booth against the wall. The waitress approached their booth and, reaching into her apron pocket, retrieved a coin and handed it to someone. Her animated gestures indicated she was speaking to a child.

"Remember, B-11," the waitress said, walking away.

The blonde slid from the booth, her back toward Eden. She was wearing a sleeveless summer dress. Before he could determine her features, the waitress intersected his line of vision as she carried the patty melt toward his table.

Setting the platter in front of him, a few French fries slid from the plate to the tabletop. "There you go, Cowboy."

Eden shot her a terrified look and appeared ready to bolt from the booth.

"It's okay, hon. I didn't mean to accuse you of nothin'," she said. "Ain't that what they call you folks from Wyoming?"

"Yes," he said, still staring at her. He could feel his hands begin to tremble as he searched her eyes for additional recognition. He had not been called Cowboy since Vietnam.

"You know, we used to have an ear of corn on our license plates," she said, somewhat reflective. "I liked that. It gave us some identity like your buckin' horse and cowboy." She nodded toward the window.

Eden turned to see his Willys parked at the curb with the prominent Wyoming logo centered on the license plate below the winch.

"Can I get you another Pepsi, hon?"

"No thanks. I'm fine," he said, turning back and attempting to look around her toward the woman across the room.

"Can I get you anything else right now?"

"No, this will do it for now. Thanks," he said, again attempting to look around her.

The waitress turned her head to see what had distracted him. Turning back, she gazed at him for several seconds but did not speak. The room suddenly exploded with the shrill twang of a steel guitar and the voice of Hank Williams.

Hey-hey good lookin'
Whatcha got cookin'?
How's about cookin'
Somethin' up with me?

The gaudy Wurlitzer faced the dining area from just outside the kitchen door. A small area in front of the jukebox served as a makeshift dance floor. At its center was the most beautiful woman Eden had ever seen. She was dancing with the little girl.

Hey sweet baby,
Don't you think maybe,
We could find us
A brand new recipe?

The waitress and several philodendron-covered posts blocked his view. He was forced to lean conspicuously to his right in order to see her. The dance was a combination of boogie- woogie and a well-rehearsed, synchronized pantomime. The little girl was four or five years old, her blonde hair pulled into a ponytail. She watched the woman intently, her actions delayed slightly as she took her cues from her partner.

I got a Hot Rod Ford
And a two dollar bill
And I know a spot
Right over the hill

There's soda pop
And the dancin's free
So if you wanna have fun
Come along with me

Say-hey good lookin'
Whatcha got cookin'?
How's about cookin'
Somethin' up with me?

They cupped their hands around their mouths to mime "Say-hey." Placing their left hands on their hips they gave exaggerated wiggles while rotating the forefingers of their right hands in imaginary dimples of their cheeks with Shirley Temple cuteness. "Cookin'" was represented by a make-believe mixing bowl under one arm, stirred with the other. The subject of each stanza had a corresponding gesture that had been well-choreographed.

The woman was tall and slender. Her arms and muscular calves were tan. Wide-set eyes separated by a perfect nose above a heart-stopping smile transfixed Eden. The little girl was equally beautiful. She, too, wore a summer dress. Her dark arms and legs were marred by mosquito bites and the scabs of an active childhood. Both wore new, white sneakers that contrasted with their tanned ankles, providing surreal movement to their synchronized dance steps. Eden stared shamelessly at them. He realized it was something more than the woman's flawless beauty that attracted him. It was the Rockwell-like image of a mother and daughter laughing and dancing in a small Midwestern café that held his gaze. He could not swallow. His hands began to tremble again. He wanted to talk with her, but knew he could not. He wanted to confide in her, tell her of the unforgivable things he had done, hold his head to her breast and sob deeply while awake. He wanted to seek absolution from the angelic figure, certain she was the only person who could grant it.

The music stopped and the mother hugged the daughter to her and spun in a circle; the little girl's legs swung perpendicular to the floor. The lunchroom crowd applauded, someone whistled, and the waitress yelled, "Yeah, Jessica! That was great, hon. You've got a regular Rockette on your hands, Beth."

Turning back toward Eden, the waitress looked at him and folded her arms across her chest. "Earth to Cowboy," she said, waving a hand in front of his face.

"Excuse me," Eden said.

"Show's over. You're about to drool. You know, your eyeballs will dry out if you don't blink once in a while."

Eden blushed and looked down at his untouched plate.

"It's okay, Cowboy. I'm just teasing you a little. Beth's a real looker. Could have been a movie star or a beauty queen. Educated, too, got a degree in something about agriculture or economics or some such nonsense." She turned and looked at the woman and sighed. "Tell ya one thing. If I had her looks, I'd of blown this shit hole a long time ago."

Surprised at her description of Rockwell's America, Eden looked up at her.

"Sorry," she said, her eyes searching his. "Eat your food, Cowboy. She's married." The waitress turned on her heel and walked toward the elderly couple.

The woman and child made their way to the door. The woman issued greetings and thanks to the other patrons, calling them by name. Her voice was deep, a sensual alto that Eden thought odd for a willowy blonde. She glanced at Eden and smiled shyly, perhaps embarrassed by his presence. Eden mustered half a smile in return while quickly looking away.

The bells above the door tinkled and she was gone. He could breathe again. Turning, he saw her standing on the sidewalk in front of the café. She was talking to greasy Les from the Texaco station. Les gestured with his thumb to the Willys and then nodded toward the restaurant. She looked over her shoulder and met Eden's stare through the café window. This time he did not look away. A breeze swept several strands of hair across her expressionless face. She brushed them aside without taking her eyes from his. Turning back, she smiled and nodded to Les and walked away, taking the little girl's hand in hers.

CHAPTER 6

"All was ended now, the hope, and the fear,
and the sorrow,
All the aching of heart, the restless,
unsatisfied longing,
All the dull, deep pain, and constant
anguish of patience!"
Henry W. Longfellow
Evangeline

5:40 a.m.

SHE COULD HAVE BEEN ANYONE. He was glad it was her. He never dreamed it would turn out this way. But, there had been no plan. Eden straightened the picture on the bookshelf and gently felt the smoothness of the walnut frame. It was of Elizabeth, taken shortly after their marriage. She was climbing up the ladder to the cab of the huge John Deere combine. Looking over her shoulder, she was smiling, a toothy grin that forced a smile in return, even a quarter century later. He had never planned to love her.

Eden had planned very little in his life. He was content to ebb and flow with the currents that surrounded his existence. There was no destiny. He thought it ironic that he would now plan so carefully. But there were no alternatives. Even if there were, he had decided not to accept them. He was tired of the guilt, tired of the nightmares. He loved Beth too much.

Congress had moved quickly, forced by the media to assign blame. The television news media had been most aggressive as the networks competed for sponsors and viewers. They developed theories that were plagiarized within minutes by their peers and presented as facts in the frenzy of media coverage that followed the disclosure. Each network paraded out panels of experts, university professors with bow ties and degrees in political science to respond to each other and the self-indulgent news anchors. The Democrats were eager to start the fight. They had lost control of both the House and Senate in the last election and needed a good GOP scandal to elevate their self-esteem. But, more importantly, they wanted the White House. To get it, they needed to discredit the leading contender for the GOP presidential nomination, Senator Winston Tucker of North Carolina. That was made easy by Tucker lying during the congressional inquiry. The donnybrook that followed was predictable. Senate Minority Whip, John Roberts of Michigan, was positioning himself as the Democratic contender. The good Senator had staked his political future on exposing Tucker's involvement in helping Nixon with a massive Republican cover-up during the Vietnam war. Roberts had chaired the Joint Oversight Committee on Military Affairs until the Republicans had taken control. He smelled a political rat the size of Winston Tucker. Exposing Tucker as Nixon's henchman in killing American pilots to cover-up Nixon's defiance of Congress was Robert's political brass ring. The lynch mob mentality of outraged MIA/POW groups and the incessant speculation of the media left little choice but for Congress and the White House to investigate.

Winston L. Tucker had risen meteorically in Republican politics. His military career was equally impressive, having been the Air Force's youngest brigadier general in history. He had left the Air Force early, before the war had ended, when

Nixon had asked him to head the National Security Administration. He was appointed Secretary of Defense for a brief two years, filling out the unexpired term of Secretary Summers, who had resigned amid allegations of military contractor kickbacks. He'd disappeared into the private sector during the Carter administration, then ran for the Senate during the Reagan years on an ultra-conservative platform, while wooing the tobacco industry and the religious right. His campaign war chest allowed him to outspend any congressional candidate in American history.

Washington insiders knew of the special bond between Tucker and Nixon. Some assumed that Tucker had helped Nixon defy Congress with the bombings of Cambodia and Laos late in the war. But when Roberts' people had discovered LaFollette, a full-blown political battle had erupted. Spurred on by the National League of POW/MIA Families, President Clinton allowed thousands of documents to be declassified. Falsification of records had been rampant and Tucker's name was all over them.

Veterans and POW/MIA groups were eager to inflame the public. The Clinton administration, they believed, had taken away U.S. leverage to pressure Hanoi for information on the POW/MIA issue. Clinton had lifted the trade embargo, assigned a U.S. Ambassador to his newly established embassy in Hanoi, and forged a bilateral trade agreement. They believed the current administration could help undo those injustices by supporting a Congressional inquiry.

Both sides had spent inordinate amounts of time on the process, each positioning for power and public support. The Whitewater and Lewinsky scandals of the Clinton administration were still fresh in the minds of the public. The Chief of Investigations for the Justice Department spent two weeks attempting to justify his selection of the Head of the Investigation

Task Force. Two more weeks of partisan bickering ensued when a special prosecutor was named. Enough political pressure developed from media-fueled public outrage that a grand jury was seated. A middle-aged farmer from Iowa had been summoned by the jury.

Eden picked up the newspaper from the hall table and held it to his nose. The smell of newsprint that he once found refreshing now produced fear. The headline on the day-old Des Moines Register read: "NIXON ORDERED COVER-UP." The sub-heading stated, "Grand Jury Hears Claims of Tucker Involvement." The lead story was titled: "Covert Special Forces Implicated" followed by "SOG Members to Testify."

The coffee shop talk at the co-op was mixed, but the general sentiment was to leave it all alone. They agreed that Vietnam was a blemish in American history and wanted to know what good it would do to dredge up the mistakes of a fallen, dead president.

Elizabeth had not mentioned the issue. He liked the fact that she, like him, was apolitical. They eagerly tracked the policies of the Secretaries of Agriculture and the U.S. Trade Ambassador, but little more. She had the wonderful ability to shrink the world around her. Only what she could touch was important.

Jessica was the activist. She found a cause to go along with every perceived injustice. Eden believed that her privileged childhood and sheltered life allowed her the luxury of caring. In contrast, Vietnam had robbed him of compassion. He quietly ranked each of the societal injustices against the savage inhumanity of war. Most seemed trivial in comparison. The distant, unsympathetic look in his eyes when Jessica was on her soapbox infuriated her. "You just don't get it, do you?" was her favorite final word on an issue. He preferred to play the role of being the unenlightened, uninspired dirt farmer, rather than burden her with his justification for apathy. But it bothered him that Jessica knew more about an endangered toad or the plight of the homeless than she did about the man who had raised her. Now she would never know.

He placed the newspaper back on the table and walked to the living room window. The sun had moved several feet down the face of the barn. The glint of something reflective flashed from beyond the cornfield where the driveway intersected the county road. He strained to see in the uncertain light between the dancing blades of corn along the fence row. Again there was the flash of something metallic. Eden quickly moved to the kitchen, plucking his binoculars from the coat hook next to the mud porch door. Leaning over the sink he brought the glasses to focus on the fence corner a quarter mile distant. The mail box, the Farm Bureau member sign, the Pioneer Hybrids sign all materialized. The chrome molding of a windshield flashed electrically, startling him momentarily so that he lost the image. Finding it again, his hands began to tremble as he attempted to focus on the two forms in the front seat. He stepped back involuntarily with the discovery that the passenger was staring back at him with binoculars.

"Sons-a-bitches," he whispered. But he was not surprised. They had shown up in town the day before. Parked across from the feed store, they had watched him when he went in to pay off his credit account. The Alamo rental car with Polk County license plates from Des Moines was obvious. He doubted if there was another Mazda within fifty miles.

His heart raced as he moved to the mud porch door and peered from between the lace curtains and through the lilac bushes that surrounded that end of the house. The white sedan was even more visible from this vantage point. *Why in the hell are those guys wearing coats and ties at a quarter to six in the morning?* he asked himself. He was more surprised by their conspicuousness than their presence. He had known they would come. Over thirty years had passed since he'd left the Army. These guys had been in diapers, if even born, when he had been strafing the jungles of Southeast Asia. *The government never forgets.* They knew where to find him. They had always known. He had signed his life away after a week of debriefing more than three decades ago. They had kept reminding him of everything they wanted him to forget. He agreed to never take a polygraph test without their presence or visit any of nineteen listed countries. He had been amused by the stipulation that if he were to ever fly over those countries that the plane have at least two engines and be equipped with parachutes. Why would they want him to survive a crash? He was a liability, not an asset. The agreement had been upheld, but he was clearly a liability. He had never discussed with anyone what he knew. He had been a good soldier, then and now. But they wanted to remind him of his oath. Why else would they be so obvious? *That's it*, he thought. *They just want to intimidate me, to let me know that they can take me out whenever they want. They know about the subpoena and want to make sure I keep my mouth shut.* "Not to worry, assholes," he said.

Why me? he thought as he walked back into the shadows of the living room. *Why so much attention to an E-5 door gunner? What about the brass? What about the chopper pilots? What about the guys in the rear like Ivan*? He wondered if Ivan was still alive. Did he receive a summons to testify? He had never attempted to contact him when he had gotten stateside. Of course he never contacted anyone. That period of his life was blank, deleted from any conversation or reference to the past.

What about LaFollette, Mr. Credibility? He'd probably sold the story to the rookie reporter who had gotten lucky when he'd approached Roberts. The Senator was looking for something to hang his political hat on. They obviously had more than the ranting of a homeless doper from the Mall, but they needed someone to corroborate his story—someone more credible than that crazy Cajun LaFollette. The media could smell Tucker's blood. Veterans groups and POW/MIA organizations staged impromptu rallies whenever a television news team drove by. They would burn the memory of Nixon at the stake and expose Tucker. They needed Eden Cain to testify. The presidency of the United States hung in the balance.

Eden stared at the familiar trademarked logo of Smith and Wesson inlaid in silver on the checkered walnut grip of the revolver. The superimposed W over the S was also stamped into the receiver. Their names were spelled out on one side of the stubby two-inch barrel. On the other side it said .38 S.&.W Spl. Inside, a rounded chunk of lead—covered with copper in order to control expansion—was primed and charged. He knew how it worked. Penetration was important but had to be balanced with the need for mushrooming in the soft tissues. The images played in slow motion over and over again in his mind. He had killed so many people. Some so close that he could see the spray of blood and bone fragments spewing explosively from behind them. It was so easy. All he had to do was point and pull the trigger; the gun exploded the round and directed the bullet. It was the bullet that did the killing. Just be the eyes for the machine and squeeze. Like falling off a log, that simple. Point and pull. The bullet does the killing. Copper-jacketed death.

CHAPTER 7

"All that we see or seem is
but a dream within a dream."
Edgar Allan Poe
A Dream Within a Dream

1974

ASPHALT HEAT WAVES WARPED THE AIR ABOVE THE abandoned street. Cottonwood spores drifted lazily among the distortions, slowly animating the still afternoon. The image was never expected. At night, he would force himself to the surface of consciousness by screaming. During the day, the hallucination seized him, a possession that commanded all his senses. Reality suspended.

The runner rounded the corner from a block away. He ran down the center of the street in exaggerated slow motion, straight toward Eden. The world became silent except for the dull, rhythmic whoosh of the main rotor from somewhere in the background. It was in synchrony with the hollow thumping of Eden's heart resonating from within his heaving chest. The runner's flight suit was torn and caked with mud. His fists were clenched tightly as his arms pumped slowly skyward. The tendons of his neck were taught against his skin. His mouth was agape, gulping air as he raced between the muzzle flashes from behind him. Muscular legs pumped powerfully toward Eden, mud flying from the soles of his boots. The fear on his face was that of a man falling but determined to right himself in an attempt to survive the impact. He did not speak. His eyes told the story. He wanted to live.

The siren's cry sped toward him from afar, dissipating the apparition when it arrived with earsplitting force. It was noon and the August heat of Iowa reminded him of what he wished to forget. Eden wiped the sweat from his brow with the back of his hand. He wished a lot lately. He wished he would stop seeing what he had seen nearly every day for three years. During the day the vision was disturbing, even frightening. At night it was terrifying. The fat landlady who lived above his basement apartment had asked if he was sleeping well. He assumed she had heard his screams in the night.

He tossed the last bag of horse chow into the back of the truck from the loading dock.

"Eden, better grab a quick sandwich," Mr. Schaeffer said, leaning from the door of the feed store. "Carl Peterson just called from the Ford garage and he's on his way over with a list of things he wants delivered this afternoon."

Looking down at the front of his sweat-stained T-shirt, Eden said, "I'm fine, Mr. Schaeffer. I'll catch a bite later." As with most days, Eden had not packed a lunch. Sometimes he would walk to the corner grocery and buy anything made by Hostess or a can of sardines. On hot days he would often buy a can of ripe olives, eat the olives, and drink the juice. He wiped the back of his neck and face with his bandanna and ran his comb through his wet hair. The prospect of making a delivery to the Peterson farm made his heart race. He was suddenly more concerned about his appearance than his stomach.

Elizabeth Peterson would occasionally stop at the feed store with her father's precise list of needed supplies. She was confident and to the point. Eden thought she was a little too direct and that was why he felt intimidated in her presence. "How do you like Iowa?" she once asked him. "What do you think of Iowans? What about Iowa women? Have you ever had an intelligent conversation with a blonde, Swedish, Catholic, Iowa farm girl?" She seemed to delight in gently probing him. She never allowed him to finish a sentence or return a question. Instead she would smile and walk away, her blue eyes flashing and blonde ponytail wagging. He could not tell if she was flirting with him or mocking him; he assumed it was the former. He still believed she was the most beautiful human on the planet, but he feared being around her.

The Amish made him nervous, too. When Mr. Schaeffer had given him the job, he'd stressed the importance of being courteous to his Amish customers. Prior to his arrival in Keotonka, he had never met an Amish person. Eden knew about horses and remembered feeding cattle loose hay in the winter from a sled pulled by giant Belgian draft horses that his father had trained. The Amish loved their horses and would respond to his compliments and questions concerning their animals. But most of the time they were politely noncommunicative and stoic as Eden loaded their buggies or wagons. Mr. Schaeffer said they minded their own business. The waitress at the cafe was fond of saying, "They wouldn't say shit if they had a mouthful."

Carl Peterson's white pickup rolled gently to a stop in front of the feed store. Eden left the loading dock to greet him.

"Afternoon, Mr. Peterson," he said through the open driver's side window.

"Hi ya, Eden," Carl Peterson said. "How come you're all wet? Can't take this Iowa heat, eh? I'll bet it doesn't get this hot in Wyoming." Like his daughter, he liked to ask rapidfire questions that probed Eden's newcomer status.

"No, sir. But I'll weather it all right."

Carl Peterson had taken an immediate liking to Eden Cain. Mr. Schaeffer had introduced them on his first day at

Keotonka Feed. Carl was a handsome, well-groomed man of about sixty with a full head of pure white hair. He and Elizabeth shared the same warm smile. Reddish-brown blotches along his hairline and on the backs of his hands told of his fair complexion as a young man and a life of working outdoors.

"You stay out of that sun else you'll end up looking like me, an old Dalmatian. I'm on my way up to the skin doctor at Burlington now. He has to cut and burn all that sun off me."

"Sorry to hear that, Mr. Peterson."

"Thought I'd stop at the Massey Ferguson dealership long as I'm there and check out one of those new grain drills you were talking about. Been reading about them some. I don't know if folks in this part of the country are ready for minimum tillage practices. I read in a magazine that in a few years they'll have a new drill out that requires no tillage. You don't even sweep or run a rod weeder over the field first, just drill the seed straight into the stubble and residue and apply a little chemical for weeds. What would folks say about a man who had such trashy looking fields?"

Eden smiled at him and said, "They'd say you are ahead of your time, Mr. Peterson. Greater yields, better soil moisture, less diesel, virtually no erosion, less compaction, less run-off, less time. Believe me, in not too many years the folks that blacktop their fields in the fall will be viewed as poor farmers and there'll be a bronze statue of you in the park."

"I've done pretty well for myself without much help from the college boys," Carl said, squinting proudly at Eden.

"Yes you have, but it's the next generation that we have to worry about. When you lose your topsoil and contaminate your groundwater, where will we be?" Eden smiled and squinted back at him.

"You're just like my daughter. Goes off to college and comes back with a head full of crazy ideas. Since her mother died, she's all I got now, so I have to listen. Here," he said, handing Eden a scrap of paper. "I'm going to be late for my appointment. Could you pull this stuff together and deliver it to the farm? Elizabeth will show you where to put it."

"I'll do it right away, Mr. Peterson."

"Say that's a nasty scar on your arm, Eden. What'd the other guy look like?"

Eden looked down at the broad band of raised flesh across his upper arm. "He's dead, Mr. Peterson." He turned to stare directly into Carl Peterson's eyes. "I killed him," he said, smiling.

Carl stared back at him, shocked by the answer, not knowing how to interpret Eden's matter-of-fact response. "I forget you're from Wyoming. Guess that's how you do it out west," he said, smiling back at Eden, his blue eyes sparkling.

"At noon in the middle of Main Street, everybody turns out," Eden said.

Carl smiled broadly. "I've got to run. Thanks, Eden. Tell that old crook, Schaeffer, to put it on my tab."

"I'll take care of it. Good luck in Burlington."

*****

The low gear ratio in the rear end of the 1954 Chevy one ton caused the truck to whine loudly. The yellow gravel popped and crunched from below the dual tires on the rear of the flatbed. A plume of yellow gravel dust billowed from behind the truck, then gently drifted over the cornfields on either side of the road. Gently rolling, wooded hills rimmed the narrow river valley. Corn grew from every tillable surface. Fields were occasionally interrupted by neat farmsteads with giant oak and walnut trees in their yards. The huge farmhouses were all white, as were the barns and other outbuildings.

Some were the traditional barn red with white trim. Eden marveled at the immaculate appearances of the farms. The lawns were manicured, trees trimmed, buildings in excellent repair with an almost total lack of farm implements in view. In Wyoming he was used to seeing the complete mechanical history of a farm or ranch represented in the front yard. It was difficult to determine which farms were Amish except on wash day, when Amish yards were filled with drying clothes. Rows of white shirts, black pants and bibs, long dresses, and doily-like bonnets hung from clotheslines near the house. Black buggies and horses were usually close by. Some Amish farmers drove steel-wheeled tractors and had generators for electricity. Eden did not understand the contradictions and believed it would be rude to ask them.

Mr. Schaeffer gave him detailed directions to the Peterson farm. Eden had accepted them without question, although he knew where the farm was. On weekends he explored the countryside in his Willys, sometimes stopping to fish the deep holes next to the riverbank in the wooded corridor that followed the river. He'd discovered the Peterson farm on such an outing the month before. He had driven by the farm every weekend since.

An Amish buggy appeared ahead of him on the rusted overhead-span bridge crossing the river. The large red triangle with black capital letters spelling "SLOW" wired to the back of the buggy seemed out of place as it cautioned that a slow moving vehicle was attached. Eden slowed and stopped at the foot of the bridge, not wishing to spook the horse as it high-stepped across the wooden planking, its head held high, blinders protecting it from the scary view on either side. Looking in the rear view mirror, he ran his fingers through his hair and plucked his T-shirt from his sticky back.

He turned on the side road just past the bridge and headed upriver toward the Peterson farm. "Good afternoon, Beth. May I call you Beth? Another wonderfully cool day here in paradise, wouldn't you agree? As a Swedish, Catholic, Iowa farm girl, I was wondering, do you sweat?" he rehearsed. His lighthearted mood began to change when the barn and silo of the Peterson farm came into view. A lump formed in his throat as he softly said, "What am I doing here?" It was a question he had asked himself several times a day since arriving in Keotonka.

Eden stopped the truck at the DeKalb Genetics sign near the Peterson mailbox. He had never driven this close to the Peterson farm before. His hands left wet smudges on the black steering wheel. He took a deep breath, found first gear, and said, "Lock and load."

The farmstead was even more orderly. Everything stationary was painted. Giant, gnarled oak trees, interspersed with tall pines, surrounded the stately two-story frame home. The gambrel-roofed barn with its prow front, dormers, and twin copulas capped with glass bulb lightning rods was storybook in appearance. Two large fuel tanks perched side-by-side on stilts next to the barn were painted red. White stenciled letters proclaimed one to be diesel and the other gas. The tall, first story windows of the house were shielded by a wide wraparound porch. A porch swing hung by the front door.

He was unsure if the supplies, mostly hog supplements, were to be unloaded in the barn or in one of the other outbuildings. Mr. Peterson had said that Elizabeth would show him where to unload.

Eden opened the gate of the low, ornate wrought iron fence and made his way along a cracked sidewalk, heaved unevenly from the tree roots below. As he approached the front porch he heard music from the direction of the backyard. With long strides he made his way among the trees and lilac bushes, rounded the corner of the house, and abruptly emerged deep into the sunny backyard. The music played from a portable radio sitting on the ground next to the lawn chair in which Elizabeth lay sunbathing. She was lying on her back, facing away from him, her breasts pointing skyward. She was topless.

Startled, Jessica looked up at him from the middle of the tractor tire sandbox. In the instant before she raised her plastic shovel, pointed, and yelled, "Mommy, there's a man," Eden's options flashed before him, colliding in a jumble of terrifying outcomes. He froze. A twirling statue in a child's game, he was caught mid-stride, gloves in hand, eyes wide, mouth open. In the background he faintly heard Jessica calling out her discovery. He wanted to turn and run, but his legs belonged to someone else.

His eyes, too, belonged to another. Instead of allowing him to turn away, they held fast while they recorded every detail of the scene for posterity. Hot pink toenails matched perfectly the string bikini bottom wedged between her legs. Her flat stomach glistened from the oily lotion she had applied. Wraparound sunglasses covering her eyes looked strangely out of place on an Iowa farm. Her blonde ponytail hung over a shoulder and contrasted with the bronze skin of her arm.

The pointing, blue plastic shovel oriented her to Eden. She raised herself to an elbow and looked at him without expression. Calmly, she turned away, swung her legs over the chair, and sat up. Her flawless back appeared long without the interruption of clothes. She meticulously oriented a T-shirt in her lap then pulled it over her raised arms and head. The defined groups of muscles in her back were visible for an instant before the gray shirt descended over them. She turned off the radio. Standing, she tugged as discreetly as possible at the bikini bottom tucked deeply between her rounded buttocks. Turning and walking toward him, she removed her sunglasses.

"Eden," she said, greeting him matter-of-factly.

Only his eyes moved, nervously searching out an escape route. His throat was dry from having his mouth open. It hurt when he swallowed. "Afternoon, Beth," he finally said. "May I call you Beth?"

She stared blankly at him.

"Another wonderfully cool day here in paradise, wouldn't you agree?"

Still, she looked at him without expression.

"I was wondering if Swedish, Catholic, Iowa farm girls sweated. I mean, perspired." *What the hell am I saying*, he thought. *Did I really say that out loud*? His eyes darted again for an escape route.

"Eden, take a breath. Why are you here?" she said.

"I'm sorry, I didn't mean to see you . . . I didn't mean to barge into your backyard . . . I heard your radio, so I . . ."

"Eden," she said calmly, "why are you here?"

"I never would have come back here if I had known . . ."

"Eden, forget that," she said.

"I doubt that will ever happen," he said, looking into her eyes.

"Why are you here?"

"Supplies, your dad, delivery, truck," he sputtered, and pointed in the direction of the barn.

"I'll show you where to unload them."

"I am really, really sorry, Elizabeth."

"Shut up, Eden," she said pleasantly, then turned, walked to the lawn chair, and slipped her feet into a pair of rubber flip- flops that lay next to the radio.

He considered running for the truck. He wished this was not happening. *Please let this be a dream*, he said to himself.

Jessica stared at him with amusement. Her mouth was open and drool was about to drip from her lower lip. Eden stared back at her, hoping she would somehow break the tension.

Elizabeth extended her hand to her daughter. "Come on, honey, let's show Mr. Cain where to unload the supplies." They led the way around the house to the barn. Sand clung to the back of Jessica's legs. She periodically twisted in her mother's grasp to see if Eden was following. No one spoke. The clapping of Elizabeth's thongs on the bottoms of her feet was the only sound on that still, August afternoon. Eden was again struck by Elizabeth's beauty. He wished he had never met her. He wished he had not come to Iowa. He wished the hot pink bikini bottom that bobbed sensuously in front of him would allow him to look away.

*****

The air in the barn burned the back of Eden's mouth with each breath. Sweat dripped from his eyebrows and the end of his nose. His shirt clung to his body; a large U-shaped wet area extended downward from his chin in a darkened bib. Dust particles drifted lazily in the shaft of sunlight that streamed through the open barn door. The moldy scent of hay mingled with the leathery-sweet smell of horses and tack. He had unloaded the truck in record time, all the while cursing himself. He wanted to leave the Peterson farm and never come back. He envisioned himself stealing the feed store truck, pointing it west, and racing nonstop for the mountains of Wyoming.

He was placing the tailgate of the stake bed rack in place when Elizabeth appeared. She was wearing bibbed overalls over the T-shirt and had replaced the flip flops with lace-up tennis shoes. She held out a glass of pink lemonade, the ice cubes tinkling softly.

"Thanks," he said, removing his gloves and taking the glass from her. He emptied the glass without pause and handed it back to her. Neither of them spoke. The silence was not uncomfortable. Elizabeth turned and walked toward the house.

Eden drove slowly back to town. Again and again he saw her slowly reach for the empty lemonade glass, her diamond wedding ring sparkling softly in the subdued light.

CHAPTER 8

"His mind pictured the soldiers who would place their defiant bodies before the spear of the yelling battle fiend, and as he saw their dripping corpses on an imagined field, he said that he was their murderer."
Stephen Crane
The Red Badge of Courage

1971

JUST WHEN YOU GOT TO THINKIN' YOU WERE A MAN OF considerable influence, somebody greased your ass, eh, Captain? I see your pair of second lieuies and raise you a captain," LaFollette said, grinning broadly.

Second lieutenants were easy to come by in dead man's poker. The rules were that a captain beat a pair of second lieutenants, but a pair of first lieutenants beat a captain—but not a major or lieutenant colonel. No one had ever found a colonel or above. A single officer always beat a pair of enlisted men. Things got a little complicated when three-of-a-kind enlisted men were found or a straight flush of private through staff sergeant was established. Warrant officers were wild.

"What branch?" Eden called above the aluminum caskets.

"Army," LaFollette said.

"What if I come up with a Navy captain?"

"Same as an Army, full bird. But nobody's ever found one," LaFollette added with disappointment. "Guess that's why they're colonels."

Eden inspected another manila tag wired to the handle at the foot of a casket. DeSmet, R. J., 2LT. 778960, 2/3 Marines. A few weeks earlier, Eden had seen a picture on the front page of *Stars and Stripes* showing the last marine stepping from the plane in San Diego. Flags waved, bands played, and the American public cheered as Nixon took credit for de-escalating the conflict by bringing home the Marines. "I guess they forgot to tell you, lieutenant. You and the rest of the Second Battalion of Third Marines stationed at Da Nang," he whispered. "I've got three second lieuies to your one captain and I call you." He was tired of the morbid game invented by the enlisted air crews of the Hueys, Cobras, and Chinooks at SOG Flight Operations, headquartered fifty yards away. "Pay up, you Cajun bastard," he said as he made his way between the pallets of silver coffins. "And none of those gook Salems, either."

LaFollette met him in the center of the pole barn and tapped a nonfiltered Pall Mall Red from his pack and extended it to Eden. "Cheating cowboy," he said.

"Crazy Cajun," Eden said, taking the cigarette.

LaFollette pulled a thin joint from his breast pocket and lit it.

"Hey, man, we're on call. Don't be smoking that shit before we scramble," Eden said.

"Don't you be telling me what to do, you namby-pamby mama's boy. 'Less you want a fucking grenade rolled under your cot," LaFollette said.

Eden was not into drugs. His refusal to smoke even a joint branded him as an outsider. Some speculated that the random urine tests and hooch inspections were not random. The heavy dopers viewed him suspiciously. "Asshole," he said.

"Prick," LaFollette shot back.

They both drew on their smokes. Eden exhaled a white plume into the sticky, wet air. LaFollette held his breath and appeared to be in pain.

"Suppose these guys are embalmed?" LaFollette said, exhaling loudly.

"Got me. I doubt it. I think they're in body bags inside there. These things look pretty much airtight," Eden said.

"Reckon they reuse these aluminum caskets?"

"Yeah. Aircraft aluminum. Got to be expensive," Eden said. "I wonder if Grumman makes them."

"Well, if they ain't embalmed and the organs pierced, what happens to the gases?" LaFollette said.

Sometimes Eden was impressed with the thought processes of his new port door gunner. LaFollette had received his GED in the Army and had chosen the Army over prison. Still a PFC, he was too much of a screwup to ever achieve rank. "I suppose they pop and hiss a little when they're opened. Like a bad batch of Aunt Mable's pickles."

The pole barn with its corrugated roof looked like the one Eden's father had built to store hay. Open on all sides, it was just a tin roof supported by evenly spaced poles. Stacked to the roofline with the brushed aluminum caskets, it was a constant reminder to the chopper crews of the deadliness of war. Several times each week a C-130 transport would taxi up and forklifts would scurry back and forth, loading bodies and parts of bodies for the first segment of their eight-thousand-mile journey home. Eden wondered what they would tell Lieutenant DeSmet's family and the families of the other marines who would be killed this week and next. *Whoops, they must have missed the plane.* Or, *whoops, we forgot about the Second Battalion.*

He accepted the dying. It was the lies that made him angry. Over the course of his tour, he had developed callousness about death, his own included. Each day, he believed, would be a good day for dying. He and the other crew members faced each day with the belief that today would be the day they would be killed. No big deal. It was going to happen sooner or later. It may as well happen today. Eden understood that lack of options bred fatalism. They could not choose to stay in their hooch or catch the first plane home.

After a few months, he found that the adrenaline boost of fight or flight seldom kicked in anymore. You did your job and waited for the big one that would send you home in an aluminum box. But, he had noticed a slight change in his attitude since coloring in the tiny, numbered boxes over the breasts of the beauty on his FIGMO calendar. The calendars were started with one hundred days left in country. One was officially a short-timer when they started shading or coloring the descending order of boxes. Starting at her head, the numbered boxes worked their way down the woman's anatomy, alternating from arm to arm, down the torso, leg to leg, and finally ending with the number zero planted squarely in the center of her vagina. Fuck I Got My Orders (FIGMO) was usually bolded across the top or in a balloon above her head. Eden was now a short-timer, midway down the left leg, and he was beginning to question his mortality. The shorter he became, the more he wanted to live. With every shaded portion of her anatomy, he became more afraid of dying.

"I'm not afraid of dying," LaFollette said suddenly. "You?"

Eden looked at him and did not speak for several seconds. "Hell, yes, I'm afraid of dying. But, it's the killing that terrifies me."

The loud, electrical buzz of the scramble horn sounded from the headquarters building. Its pulsing tenor was the signal for the chopper crew to mount up. It reminded Eden of the horn the Morlocks used to call Weena and the other Eloi to the slaughter in H. G. Wells' *The Time Machine*.

"It's showtime!" LaFollette yelled above the horn. He whooped and laughed across the tarmac toward the Huey.

Eden shook his head. "Pothead," he mumbled.

*****

Lonnie Webster had said nothing about their destination or mission. They were flying high and fast, headed west, away from the sun. Eden recognized the Elephant Valley below. He guessed they were somewhere between Phu Bai and A Shau on the I Corps–II Corps boundary. If they were not over Laos, they were very close as Lonnie began his descent.

"All right, everybody; you know the drill," Lonnie said over the intercom. "We're looking for smoke and an LZ. We're landing this bird to pick up casualties."

"What the hell, over," LaFollette said. "Do we look like a Goddamn medevac? Send in those pussy nurse boys. We're a mean, lean, fightin' machine."

"Stow it, Roach Face," Lonnie said. "Just do your job."

Eden knew they got the call because a medevac crew was not SOG cleared. That and the fact that they were under-gunned, inexperienced, and somebody would miss them if they went down. If he went down in Laos, they would be scorched and listed as MIA.

The terrain was gentle, the view pastoral, as Lonnie lost altitude: yellow-green grasslands within a mosaic of puffy green jungle. Rice paddies, jumbled and narrow, contoured the landscape along the river bottoms. There were no pockmarks from bombing and artillery barrages or expanses of brown, lifeless jungle from defoliation. The country appeared, from above, to be at peace.

A plume of white smoke rose from a grassy area at the jungle's edge. Eden called it first. The chopper banked gracefully toward the clearing.

"RT Georgia, this be Pony Boy. Identify."

"It's about time, Pony Boy. This is RT Georgia's One-Two. The LZ is secure."

"Unless you identify, RT Georgia, Pony Boy will call one in on you," Lonnie said.

"Roger, Pony Boy. Stand by."

Green smoke suddenly billowed upward from the edge of the clearing.

"We confirm RT Georgia. We're coming in."

The grass waved restlessly at first, then in a frenzy, before being pushed to the ground as the Huey touched down in the clearing. Lonnie positioned the chopper with Eden facing the smoke rather than LaFollette. On the ground, Lonnie would be helpless. He'd put his life and those of his crew in the hands of his starboard door gunner. "Watch 'em, Cowboy," he said.

Eden did not respond. Both hands tightly gripped the M-60 as he scanned the edge of the clearing where the smoke was slowly disappearing. He found himself holding his breath from the tension of not seeing anything move.

"RT Georgia, Pony Boy is on the ground. Did you need an invitation?" Lonnie said.

There was no response. "Be alert, people," Lonnie said over the intercom. "I'm not liking this."

The RPM of the main rotor increased and the Huey twisted unsteadily from side-to-side as Lonnie prepared to lift off in the advent of an ambush.

"Ten seconds, RT Georgia, and I'm gone," Lonnie said.

"Hold your water, Pony Boy. This is RT Georgia's One-Zero. I'm sending my One-One and our Nung interpreter with two NVA prisoners out. Got room for four?"

"Roger, RT Georgia," Lonnie said. Four would be a tight fit. He had scrubbed the radio operator when he was told casualties were involved. They would need the space for a stretcher if necessary. "I was told you have casualties."

"Roger that, Pony Boy. We'll manage. These gooks are higher priority. Here they come."

The dark figures emerged from the jungle a hundred yards north of the smoke. That was a new one on Eden. He knew that coordinates were often given two hundred yards south of the recon team's actual position due to the NVA's monitoring of radio transmissions. The chopper ratcheted to port with Eden facing the oncoming men. The small, hatless, dark-haired figures in front had their hands behind them. Behind them, a large man in nondescript camo fatigues and a boonie hat pushed them along with the barrel of his Swedish K. Bringing up the rear was a similarly dressed Nung, round-faced and stocky, consistent with his Chinese ancestry. Trackers and fierce fighters, the Nungs were renowned mercenaries.

The American had no indication of rank or name on his uniform. He had the same square jaw and steely eyes that Eden believed to be a genetic trait of SOG members. Without a war, he believed they would be either criminals or hockey players. Without speaking, he handed his rifle to the Nung and tossed the two NVA into the chopper. Eden saw that their hands were bound tightly with wire. Blood dripped from their wrists and discolored fingers. One was a Dai-uy, a captain, whose right eyebrow was cut deeply and swollen over his eye. Blood and dirt were caked to the side of his face. Eden did not recognize the insignia of rank on the other man's uniform, but believed him to be an enlisted man. His eyes were wide with fear. His trousers were darkened down his left leg. Eden could smell the urine.

"*Dung li*, you little shits!" the American yelled.

The NVA obeyed, lying facedown on the floor behind the radio panel.

When the American and Nung were aboard, Lonnie lifted off and climbed steeply. The countryside and tension slowly disappeared as they reached altitude. Eden heard the yelling from the American and the Nung, commands or questions, some in English but most in Vietnamese. He turned to see the American holding the Dai-uy by his hair, his head pulled back unnaturally, a combat knife held to his throat. The Nung yelled the same phrase over and over, but the Dai-uy stared at him blankly with his one good eye. Suddenly the American released the Dai-uy and grabbed the NVA enlisted man. With a fluid movement and without a word, he tossed the prisoner headfirst from the starboard bay of the Huey. Eden leaned forward to watch the bound man slowly disappear below, the black dot of his body swallowed by the green earth. He turned and met the American's cold stare.

"What the fuck are you looking at?" he yelled at Eden.

Eden stared back without expression. He wondered if he, too, possessed the same cold eyes; eyes that had seen the horror of war's inhumanity, eyes that were windows to a soul without compassion. Dying was so easy. Would his eyes appear as unfeeling when killing no longer terrified him? He turned away and stared into the horizonless blue sky. He dreamed of home.

CHAPTER 9

"History is a pack of lies
about events that never happened
told by people who weren't there."
George Santayana

1974

THE GOLDEN REFLECTIONS OF COTTONWOODS SHIMmered brightly in the brown ripples of the river. The musty smell of decaying leaves grew stronger as the morning sun crept higher on the gentle bank. The October sun was warm against his outstretched body. Eden watched an ant walk the length of his fishing pole, stop at the last line guide, and peer downward. *End of the line, Mr. Ant,* he thought.

"You sure this is the spot, Carl?" Eden said without looking up. The visor of his baseball cap was pulled down over his eyes, his hands clasped behind his head.

"Sure, I'm sure. Be patient. There's catfish in that hole bigger than wiener dogs. Good eatin' size. Some say there's flatheads and blues down there big enough to drown a man," Carl said.

"Whew," Eden said, suddenly bolting upright. "Put the lid back on the stink bait, Carl, unless you want to see what I had for breakfast."

"You wouldn't last long as a hog farmer," Carl said.

"I'd kiss the south end of a northbound hog before I'd put that nasty stuff on my hook," Eden said. "Worms are what those cats like."

"We'll see." Carl smiled and cast his heavily weighted bait a few yards from shore. "That's it. Perfect."

"That's the spot, huh?"

"There's a hole there deep enough to swallow my house. When the Army Corps and the WPA built this bridge," Carl said, gesturing with his thumb toward the steel structure next to them, "they discovered it. Rumor has it that it's bottomless. They say there's an undertow out there that never gives up what it sucks down."

"Hmmmn," Eden said. He decided not to question the local legend. Carl was serious. Folklore was often stated as fact and it was considered rude for outsiders to question it. Eden liked Carl Peterson and did not wish to offend him.

"That's a fact," Carl added.

"Kind of scary," Eden said.

"How about an apple?" Carl asked, holding out a small green and red apple. "Grew 'em myself in the backyard."

"Sorry, Carl, but I don't want to eat anything that came from a hand with stink bait on it."

Carl smiled and took a bite from the apple. "Can't say as I blame you," he said, his nose wrinkled.

Carl had befriended Eden while most of the locals politely kept their distance. Their conversations revolved around tillage practices and crop genetics. Carl seemed fascinated by Eden's speculation that corn would soon be genetically altered for resistance to pests, even pesticides. Whenever he came to town he would stop by the feed store, sometimes taking Eden to the cafe for coffee. At first, Eden thought it strange that a man more than twice his age would court his friendship. Now he believed that Carl needed another man to talk with since he had only Elizabeth and Jessica at home. Nervous about the relationship, Eden had kept Carl at a comfortable distance. When Carl had discovered that Eden liked to fish, he'd invited him to his secret hole, a privilege extended to very few individuals. Caught off guard, Eden could only accept the invitation. He liked Carl and enjoyed the friendship.

"What's a smart, good-looking young man like you hanging around Keotonka for?" Carl asked without warning.

"I wish I knew, Carl. I was just passing through and stopped for lunch at the cafe. The rest is history."

"Where were you headed in the first place?"

"No place in particular. Just seeing the country. I liked what I saw here," Eden said.

"You aren't one of those draft dodgers sneaking back from Canada, are you?"

"No," Eden said, propping himself on an elbow to look at Carl. "But, if I were, would you have taken me to your secret hole?"

"Hell no, I wouldn't have. I'd of taken your sorry butt down river and dumped you so as not to pollute my secret hole. I've got no tolerance for those hippie cowards."

Eden turned away. He was surprised by Carl's tone and did not want to inflame the issue, but wanted to respond. He paused then said, "I guess I'm not sure I'd call them cowards. To leave your family, your country, to become a wanted man, to be labeled a coward takes a fair amount of courage. I sometimes wish I were as principled or convicted to a cause."

"Convicted is what they'll be if they ever set foot back in the U. S. of A.," Carl said. "It doesn't take courage to wet your pants and run. It takes courage to step up to the plate and do what needs to be done."

"Perhaps. But some folks believe this country didn't have the courage to step up to the plate. And the politicians didn't have the courage to lead. I think Vietnam was a mistake that will embarrass this country until the historians rewrite the textbooks. If I had it to do over again, I—" he caught himself, sat up and reached for his fishing pole. "I think I had a bite," he said, trying to be convincing while changing the subject.

"Let him take it good and run with it before you set the hook," Carl said. "These cats are pretty tender-mouthed. You can't horse them in unless they've swallowed the hook."

"It must have been the current," Eden said settling back.

"If you had what to do over again?" Carl said.

"Oh, nothing, forget it," Eden said.

"You're not running, are you, son?"

Eden looked at Carl for several seconds. "I guess I am, Carl. I guess I am."

"From the law?"

"No." Eden smiled and shook his head.

"From a woman?"

"No. Not that simple."

"I don't mean to pry, but—"

"Yes, you do," Eden said, cutting him off, still smiling.

"I'm just trying to figure how someone with your smarts in the prime of his life is just drifting along."

"Me too, Carl. I wish I knew where I was going. I only know where I've been. Guess I'm just trying to put time and distance between the past and whatever the future holds."

Carl sat silently. He scratched in the dirt with a stick. "Just getting your head screwed on straight, as Beth would say."

Eden laughed. "I suppose. It seems to be a little cross-threaded right now."

"Were you in Vietnam?" Carl asked suddenly.

Surprised by the question, Eden turned away and answered. "Yeah."

Carl cleared his throat in preparation for the next question, but it did not come. "I'm glad you made it back," he said finally, staring out over the slow moving river. "Some didn't."

By late morning Carl had a stringer full of eating-size channel cats. Eden reeled in and stared at the discolored remains of his original worm.

"Try some stink bait," Carl offered, holding back a grin.

Without a word, Eden accepted the offer. After baiting his hook, he was attempting to wipe the foulness from his hands on the grass of the bank when Elizabeth arrived, driving a rust-colored Studebaker pickup.

"Catch any?" she asked as she bounced down the bank, carrying a picnic basket in one hand and holding Jessica's with the other.

Eden gave her his doe in the headlights stare. He had not expected to see her. Her faded jeans clung tightly to her hips. The button fly descended sharply below her flat stomach and disappeared between her legs. She wore a baggy green sweatshirt over a white turtleneck. Her ponytail exaggerated the movements of her head as she looked between her father and Eden for a response.

Eden was speechless.

"Some of us are not doing as well as others," Carl said smugly.

"Skunked you, huh, Eden?" she said.

His mouth opened but nothing came out.

"Eden, take a breath," she said slowly. "Have you caught any fish?"

She was mocking him. He could feel his ears begin to burn with embarrassment.

"Leave the boy alone," Carl said. "Can't you see he's ashamed of himself? Not everyone can catch fish like your old dad."

"Wouldn't use the stink bait, would you?" she asked, still staring at him.

"I tried, but it's disgusting," Eden said softly, looking down.

"You wouldn't make a very good hog farmer," she said. "But I'm sure he's already told you that."

I wouldn't make a very good anything, he thought. He found her eyes and begged for mercy. Elizabeth Peterson drained him of any self-esteem he possessed. Her presence robbed him of more than speech and confidence. She exposed him by forcing him to look at himself, by reminding him of who he really was. He saw her look away as she realized his discomfort.

He had not seen her since August, when he'd surprised her while sunbathing. It was more than the voyeuristic encounter that allowed him to see through her clothes, an ability she knew he possessed, that made him blush. Being around her reminded him of the occasional dream he had of sitting at his desk in the sixth grade and realizing that he had no shoes or socks on his feet, sometimes no pants. Again, he wanted to run, to put states between Elizabeth and himself. Why did he stay here? What magnetic force held him so strongly? *Run*, he told himself. *Don't look back. Run as fast as you can. You will never be able to handle this.* Finally he spoke. "What year is that Studebaker, a fifty-one?" he asked, surprising himself with the stupidity of the question.

Elizabeth looked at him blankly.

"It's a nineteen-fifty," Carl said proudly. I bought it brand-new the year after I crossed over from Hampshires to Durocs. Those pigs took good care of us back then. Beth was only two or three at the time. We didn't even own a car, just that Studebaker."

"Here," Elizabeth said, extending a wax paper–wrapped sandwich toward Eden. "You guessed it. It's ham."

"Thanks," Eden said, his fingers lightly touching hers as he took the sandwich.

"What's that awful smell?" she teased, covering her nose with the back of her hand.

Eden blushed again, his ears ready to ignite. He wiped his hand on his jeans and nervously looked for an escape route.

"Be sure to hold the sandwich by the paper," she said.

Eden spoke in one- or two-word sentences during the course of the picnic, but only when asked a direct question. He occasionally stole glances at Elizabeth as she sat on the blanket talking quietly with Jessica and her father. He hated himself.

Elizabeth was picking up the remains of lunch when Carl said, a little too loudly, "Eden, how'd you like to join us for Thanksgiving dinner next month? We'll actually eat turkey."

Elizabeth stopped shaking the blanket and turned suddenly toward her father. She looked at Eden, then back to her father. She stood motionless.

Eden cleared his throat.

"Dad, that's more than six weeks away," Elizabeth said.

"Eden's a busy man with lots of social opportunities. Thought I'd give him plenty of notice," Carl said.

Elizabeth and Carl both stared at Eden.

"Well, thanks, Carl," Eden said. "Your invitation is very kind, but I really wouldn't want to impose upon you. Thanksgiving is a family holiday. It's for family, not strangers."

"Nonsense, you're not a stranger. You don't have any family in these parts. We'd love to have you. Wouldn't we, Beth?" Carl said.

It was Elizabeth's turn to look uncomfortable. She shot her father an angry look, then smiled at Eden. "Please come, Eden. We would love to have you."

Jessica stared at Eden without blinking.

*****

October and November passed slowly. The painter's palette of fall colors gave way to the starkness of early winter. The hardwoods stood dark and naked beneath gray skies. The dank cold chilled Eden unlike anything he had experienced in the mountains of Wyoming. Mr. Schaeffer began to refer to himself as semiretired, gradually allowing Eden to assume more responsibility in running the feed store. The locals came to accept him, as though he were a longtime member of the community. Both the Catholic priest and the Lutheran minister had made recruitment visits to the store. The Amish, respectfully, kept their distance. Carl Peterson had stopped by in mid-November. He'd been on his way to see the dermatologist in Burlington again. He had reminded Eden of the Thanksgiving dinner invitation and had not seemed in the mood to argue about it.

Thanksgiving Thursday finally arrived. The day was sunny and crisp. Eden struggled over what to wear, finally settling for corduroy trousers and a pullover sweater. He appeared relaxed but had slept little the night before. Afraid to risk having another nightmare, he got up at 4:30 a.m. and finished Sinclair Lewis' *Main Street*. He found wonderful similarities between Keotonka and the fictitious, small Minnesota towns described in Lewis' cynical novels.

The cloud of dust that trailed his Willys was interrupted by the length of the wooden planked bridge as he approached the farm. He smiled at the sight of hundreds of acres of corn stubble amid the dirt-black fields of Carl's neighbors. At Eden's urging, Carl was going to try minimum-till corn next spring. Eden had overheard some of the locals decrying the "trashy looking" fields at the Peterson place. He knew Carl was getting pressure to plow under his stubble and conform to the standards that had been passed down from previous generations.

He avoided rehearsing his lines during the drive to the Peterson farm. He would act relaxed, be mindful of his manners, and pay minimal attention to Elizabeth, who would surely goad him. On the seat next to him was a bottle of wine—of uncertain quality, since Eden rarely drank wine. A Thanksgiving sucker in the shape of a turkey, wrapped in orange cellophane, was his gift to Jessica, who always watched him suspiciously.

The scent of hog manure was strong as he waited at the front door. Carl greeted him with a firm handshake and a warm smile. Jessica disappeared with her sucker, presumably to show her mother. The aroma of cooking turkey quickly displaced the smell of pigs. The home was warm and attractive. Antique furniture, pictures of rigid relatives, ferns and lace doilies accented the large, high-ceilinged rooms. In the den, indistinguishable college football teams scrambled colorfully across the screen of a large console television. The dining room table sparkled with silver and glass atop a white tablecloth. Carl uncorked the wine and poured three glasses that he retrieved from the kitchen.

"Beth, come join us in a toast!" he called.

"Mommy!" Jessica called loudly from the center of the couch.

Carl talked excitedly about college football standings and recited the weights of Hawkeye linemen as if talking about his beloved hogs. Eden smiled and nodded, but understood little of what Carl was saying. Instead, he watched the doorway to the kitchen, feeling his pulse quicken and his palms sweat.

"Beth!" Carl yelled.

"Beth!" Jessica mimicked; she received a stern scowl from her grandfather.

Elizabeth appeared suddenly, pulling an apron over her head. She smiled as she brushed her fingers through her long hair. Her face was flushed from the heat of cooking; the pinkness of her cheeks matched the mohair sweater she wore atop black, pleated wool slacks. Eden could not breathe.

"Hi, Eden; happy Thanksgiving," she said. "I hope you're hungry because we have enough food to feed all the starving children of Missouri." She approached them quickly, took the glass of wine from her father, and—leaning toward Eden—whispered, "Take a breath, Eden."

Eden smiled broadly, nearly laughing. He shook his head and said, "Happy Thanksgiving to you, Elizabeth. You look absolutely beautiful and yes, I'm very hungry."

It was Elizabeth's turn to blush slightly.

"A toast," Carl said loudly, purposefully distracting Eden from his daughter's demureness. "To friends and family, including one beautiful daughter and granddaughter; to those present and those departed; and to the bounty of our labors."

"*Salud*," Eden said, clinking his glass against Carl's, then Elizabeth's. His eyes darted from her hand to her face and back again. She was not wearing her wedding ring. Cooking, he thought. Perhaps she had removed it while working in the kitchen.

Eden enjoyed both the dinner and the conversation. He marveled at how relaxed he had become and spoke easily in the presence of the one person who usually rendered him speechless. Several times during the meal he looked up to find Elizabeth staring at him. In most instances she was the one to look away first. By dessert, Eden observed that she had abandoned attempts to be modest and no longer looked away.

Carl talked nonstop about agriculture, politics, the economy, and the inherent laziness of poor people. "This country's cheap food policy will continue to drive people from the land," Carl said at the end of his harangue about depressed commodity prices.

"What cheap food policy are you referring to, Carl?" Eden asked. "We do have the most affordable food supply on earth; pretty diverse, too. I'm not sure I would give all the credit to the government for that. The fact that we spend less of our disposable income on food than any other nation allows us to enjoy the standard of living that we're willing to die for in order to protect. They taught me that in college, Carl."

Elizabeth was smiling from above the cup of coffee she held to her face.

Carl attempted to interrupt but Eden continued.

"It's not just about commodity prices, grain stores, or trade agreements. It's about supply and demand."

"Now you're talking," Elizabeth said flatly, clearly amused.

"My major professor used to ask if we knew when this country maximized its corn acreage," Eden said.

Carl began to swell up in preparation for a wild guess.

"Nineteen seventeen," Elizabeth said. She stared at Eden, confident in her answer.

Surprised, Eden paused and searched her eyes. "That's absolutely correct," he said. He turned toward Carl again. "We also had half our population engaged in agricultural production. I remember seeing a production curve for this century. It's almost a straight line upward into the early 1950s; it then slows a bit but still climbs right up to the present. And that curve is the inverse of acres in production and farmers on the land. My point, Carl, is that agriculture is the victim of its own success."

Carl sat silently, appearing confused. "What?" he asked, with obvious disbelief.

"Daddy, what Eden is saying is that while we have continued to produce more and more corn, we have done it on fewer and fewer acres with fewer and fewer people. Less than five percent of our population is engaged in ag production now. These efficiencies are from science, not government policy. We produce more than people want to buy. If it weren't for price support programs, we'd be down to about one percent. Government has artificially kept prices up and people on the land, just the opposite of your premise. If this were truly a free market economy, you and I would be making widgets in some factory."

"Hogwash," Carl said. "You're talking only about domestic needs. We could feed the world and get rich doing it."

"International trade policy, I think, is pretty tricky business," Eden said. "The question we have to ask ourselves is do we really want to feed the rest of the world—and why? And Elizabeth, that was the best pumpkin pie that American agriculture has ever produced," he added, in an attempt to lighten the conversation.

"Thank you, Eden," she said, still smiling at him.

"We have what we have because we work hard for it," Carl said, an obvious edge to his voice.

"Much of what we have is because we don't have to spend time hunting or gathering our food or spend most of our income for it," Eden said. "Leisure time activities, education, all the wonderful amenities of the American lifestyle are compliments of agricultural efficiencies. You're so damn good at what you do, Carl, that you have the luxury of sitting around and complaining about it."

"I don't know whether I've been complimented or insulted," Carl said.

"How about religion, Daddy, you want to discuss that one for a while?" Elizabeth asked.

"You young people are all alike," Carl said.

"Products of your efficiencies," Eden shot back.

"Boys," Elizabeth cautioned. "Let's talk about something that aids digestion. Would anyone care for more pie?"

"Me," Jessica said, whipped cream smeared around her mouth.

Everyone laughed and Carl slid his chair back, indicating the meal and the debate had ended.

"Play chess, Eden?" Carl asked.

"Yes, sir, but it's been a while."

"As soon as I check the scores and digest a bit, I'll give you a lesson."

"That means he's going to sit in his chair and sleep like a tyrannosaur that just ate a pterodactyl with all the trimmings," Elizabeth said.

"You'll need a little nap, Carl, before you play me," Eden said, smiling.

Eden helped Elizabeth clear the table and do the dishes. The conversation was light. He listened to her remembrances of Thanksgivings when her mother and grandparents were alive. Her eyes sparkled and the corners of her mouth turned upward as she stared out the kitchen window while recounting pleasant times. Eden had to remind himself to look away occasionally, for fear of being accused of gawking. He was fascinated by the small, raised line of flesh in the center of her upper lip that divided it into equal halves. He studied the graceful lines of her neck that disappeared beneath the softness of her pink sweater. He remembered her breasts. He noted the fine, blonde hairs on her arms and was intrigued by her delicate hands with long fingers.

"Eden, you're staring," she said.

He did not respond.

"Eden," she repeated sharply.

"Huh? Excuse me," he said.

"Take a breath. You're staring at me again."

"No, I wasn't."

"What was I just talking about?" she challenged.

"How would I know? I was staring at you and not listening."

"You weren't thinking about me sunbathing last August, were you?"

"No," he said quickly, looking away.

"Liar!"

Eden was silent for a moment. "Have you ever noticed that you delight in putting me on the spot? That you enjoy confronting me and making me feel uncomfortable?"

She did not answer. Instead she turned away and stared through the window into the distance.

"Like holding an insect on its back and plucking out its legs, one at a time," he added.

Turning back to him she said, "I'm sorry, Eden. I—" she hesitated, but continued to look at him, her eyes searching his. "I need to check on Jessica," she said finally, and walked from the kitchen, tossing her apron over a chair.

The chess game lasted nearly two hours. Carl played at a level that Eden had never experienced. In the end, Eden gave up any hope of an offense and was forced to defend his king with every move. He was relieved when Carl finally eliminated his options and declared checkmate.

"College boys," Carl said, pleased with his win.

"Next time I'll cut you no slack because of your age," Eden said.

Elizabeth sat on the couch reading quietly to Jessica, who looked very sleepy.

Eden looked outside, then at his watch. "It's dark and I've stayed longer than I should have," he said.

"Nonsense, we've enjoyed it," Carl said.

"I should be on my way," Eden said. "Thanks so much for allowing me to spend Thanksgiving with you. The dinner was great. I had a good time. In the future you might consider letting your guests win at chess as a matter of courtesy."

"I'm not that courteous," Carl said.

"Dad, will you take Jessica upstairs and get her bath ready? I'll see Eden out," Elizabeth said.

"I don't want to take a bath," Jessica complained.

"No arguments, young lady. Go with your grandpa," Elizabeth said.

Carl shook Eden's hand and thanked him for coming, then took Jessica by the hand and led her upstairs.

Elizabeth walked with Eden onto the porch, closing the door behind her. The early evening air was brisk.

"Beginning to feel a little like winter," Eden said, turning to face her.

Elizabeth leaned forward and kissed him, tenderly at first, then with intense emotion, her hands caressing his face. It was a deep and lasting kiss, her mouth opening and closing with the gentle swaying of her head.

Eden was caught totally off guard. Both his mind and heart raced. He stood there awkwardly accepting her kiss, but not returning the passion.

Elizabeth broke off the kiss and looked down, her head bowed, afraid to look at him. She covered her face with her hands and sobbed deeply.

He put his arms around her and pulled her tightly against his chest. She did not resist. He stroked the back of her head and held her face to his neck. He did not speak. Her back convulsed with stifled sobs. Slowly she regained her composure and gently pushed herself away from him. Still, she did not look at him. Her bottom lip quivered and tears stained her cheeks. She turned and silently disappeared into the house.

*****

Eden stopped the Willys on the bridge and got out. Leaning over the iron rail he watched the black water pass slowly beneath him. The currents roiled. Agitated whirlpools arose from the bottomless hole, swirling reminders of the undertow that lurked beneath the surface. With his foot, he scuffed a few pieces of gravel from the wooden planking into the water. The splash was muffled and the rings quickly disappeared into the turbid blackness. The disturbance was over so quickly, so quietly, and without a trace. Small shards of limestone returned to the water that once covered them. Home at last, embraced by the silent coolness of their birth.

He did not remember the trip back to Keotonka. He sat on the edge of his bed in the darkness of the basement apartment. The scattered remnants of his life swirled above him, caught in the undertow of his consciousness. Sleep was the bottomless pit. At 2:27 a.m. the dull resonance of the Huey's main rotor faded into the depths below him as he struggled to the surface for air.

CHAPTER 10

"Wasn't it a funny dream!—
perfectly bewild'rin'!—
Last night, and night before, and
night before that."
James Whitcomb Riley
"Dream-March"

5:47 a.m.

EDEN HAD TRIED FOR YEARS TO FORGET. Sometime in his early forties he gave up. The realization that he would never get his youth back was acceptable. What broke him was the awareness that he would never outlive the memory of Vietnam. No amount of distraction, pleasure, or hardship could bury those scattered moments that had changed his life. The past was reality; the present was based on it. Only the future was uncertain. He was uncertain about life after death, but he lacked absolute proof. Death was a gamble. Eternal memory was surely damnation. He hoped for the numbed finality of extinction.

The softness of dawn spread with a pink glow down the wall of the hallway, illuminating the framed exhibition of family history. He smiled at the photograph of Elizabeth and Jessica—dressed in shorts and T-shirts—throwing snowballs at each other in July, with Lake Marie and the Snowy Range in the background. Eden had taken them to Wyoming only once. It was after his parents had died. His mother had gone first, just two years after he'd left Wyoming. John Cain died at the same time, but his body had lingered on for another decade. He had sold the ranch to a large Colorado corporation who allowed him to live on the home place until his death. The corporation granted one last burial in the family cemetery, then cut off all access to the ranch. Corporate executives, their jets parked in Saratoga, hunted and fished the ranch on weekends.

On rented horses, Eden had taken Elizabeth and Jessica to the only part of his past that remained. During the summers of his high school years he had illegally built a log cabin in the most remote corner of the national forest. His family had held the grazing lease for three generations. Eden had discovered the valley while gathering cattle one fall. It was the most obscure piece of real estate in Wyoming. Even the aerial photographs at the district ranger's office showed it as a shadow between the rugged mountains that surrounded it.

The site was reached by only one trail that came from above, a treacherous rocky ledge with blind curves, so narrow that horses had to be led. The valley floor faced south, with old-growth Engelmann Spruce shielding the small stream that disappeared underground three hundred yards from its beginning. Eden had never found evidence that miners or loggers had discovered the valley. He had felled standing dead spruce, hand-peeled them, dragged them by horse to the cabinsite, and lifted them with block and tackle from log tripods. Everything, from windows to shingles, had been hauled in by pack horse. Even the old wood cookstove had been painstakingly packed in a piece at a time. He'd milled the floor planks and even insulated the ceiling. On holidays and school breaks from college, he would disappear into the mountains to continue his work. After Vietnam, he discovered it was the only place on earth where he did not have the nightmares.

Elizabeth and Jessica were the only people that Eden had taken into the valley. Until then it had always been Eden's secret, but it was one secret he could give up. Elizabeth was awestruck by the scenery and Eden's handiwork. Jessica loved the storybook seclusion of the cabin and valley, and seemed convinced that gold or lost Spanish treasure was buried there. The drive back to Iowa was unusually quiet as they each reflected on the five days they had spent in the solitude of nature. Elizabeth would occasionally squeeze Eden's hand and smile. She was happy. They made plans for returning every year. Fifteen years had passed and they had not returned.

He, too, had been happy. Now, he could not explain the way he felt about Elizabeth. So much of the passion had turned to pain with the arrival of the letter. The relationship had always been tempered. After twenty-nine years of marriage, neither of them truly knew the other. They were good at predicting each other's reactions. They knew each other's idiosyncrasies and knew how to please or anger each other. The marriage was based on friendship and mutual support, but had always been aloof. Their pasts were inviolable, a sacredness that each respected. There were times that he wished he could go back in time, to change the past in order to influence the present.

But, it would have meant a very different life, a life without Elizabeth and Jessica. They were his life. From the moment he first saw her dancing in the café, he had devoted his life to her. There were no personal ambitions. He was content to be obscure, an insignificant person who constantly feared exposure. Fanfare and recognition were to be avoided. He only wanted to be a good husband and father. He now accepted his burden and carried the load with resolve. Everything in his life paled in comparison to that burden. Vietnam had taken something from him, but it also had given him perspective, aided by the daily and nightly reminders of the war he could not forget. He believed he was a gentler person as a result.

The hall clock seemed unusually loud, competing with the hollow thumping of his heart. He touched another photo of Elizabeth and Jessica and tried to swallow the grief that formed in his throat. He attempted to suppress the wish that he had never come to Iowa so many years ago. It lingered there, attempting to overlay reality. There had been no plan; life just happened a day at a time. Now there was a plan, but he had not counted on the Feds showing up. From the kitchen window he lifted the binoculars and glassed the sedan again. The driver appeared familiar; either Eden had seen him before or knew someone who looked like him. Where? and who? were the questions that raced through his mind. He resented the Feds' presence and the distraction they created. *Focus*, he thought; he must focus on the task at hand.

The sun drew a line between light and dark above the barn door. The fuel tanks were turning red with color, their white labels contrasting in the morning light. Eden turned back to the large tanks on their rusted stilts. The cap on the diesel tank dangled from the end of its chain. The Co-op truck had been there the day before to deliver fuel. Eden had paid little attention except to ask the driver where Ernie was; he had been told that Ernie was sick and that the new driver was substituting for him. Eden always made it a point to talk with Ernie and show him some attention.

Fifteen years earlier, Ernie had been the local football hero. Keotonka, like many small towns, rallied their support for high school athletics. Young men with limited talent became short-term celebrities. Cheerleader girlfriends drifted away when the college scholarships failed to arrive. A once-230-pound mass of muscle with electric reflexes now delivered diesel fuel or propane, his first name embroidered within an oval patch on the shirt that barely covered his ponderous belly. Ernie was the poster child for has-been athletes.

Local farmers no longer patronized him by mentioning the district championship game from fifteen years earlier. But Ernie still strutted, acting as if he expected the head coach from the University of Iowa to call at any moment. Eden did not know the second string delivery man and had paid little attention to him. *No wonder he's second string*, he thought, *he forgot to put the cap back on the fill spout.* If it had rained during the night, the entire tank would have been contaminated. He would put it back on when he went to the barn. Elizabeth did not need any additional complications.

He glassed the Feds again. One of the men stood at the rear of the car facing the opposite direction. He was urinating. *What do they want with me at six in the morning?* Eden asked himself. Were they waiting to knock on his door after breakfast and expose him? Maybe they were not FBI. Maybe they were from the Justice Department and were here to serve another subpoena or to make sure he did not run. Perhaps they were Army and wanted to remind him of his oath. Whoever they were, they filled Eden with a sense of urgency, a last-minute complication that threatened his plan.

He walked quickly to the office and stood in the middle of the room, unsure of what to do next. Elizabeth knew where everything was. She had always taken care of the financial records and legal documents. The file cabinet was filled with neatly labeled folders, everything in its place. There was no need to pull the appropriate documents. She would know what to do. His legal instructions were simple and specific with little room for interpretation. Besides, there was no one to argue about it. Jessica would never challenge her mother.

He was not afraid; it would be simple. He was sad. Sad that he lacked the courage to tell Elizabeth about the horrors that plagued him, sad that he had not confided in her. The truth had become more elusive with each passing year, more difficult to accept, more difficult to explain. He had rehearsed his confession a thousand times and considered her every response. Invariably, she would understand. Life would go blithely on with the heavy burden of guilt cast aside, their bond strengthened by disclosure. He knew that Elizabeth loved him. She had always loved him. It was not a marriage of convenience. Nor was it a marriage of divulgence. There was so much unsaid. Eden had always regretted his inability to communicate his feelings to his wife, though he outwardly appeared to take pride in his stoicism.

How unfortunate, he thought, *there's so much to say*. Life had been a wasted opportunity to express himself, his feelings repressed by fear, masked by machismo. He was not much better expressing himself in writing than he was talking. He could write her an explanation, an apology, or tell her how much he loved her; but it would read like a standard business letter. *Why change now*? he reasoned. He wished he could change who he was, but it was too late. *Accept it and stay in character, do not make this harder on her than it has to be*, he thought.

He was stalling. Standing in the middle of the room, he did not know what to do next. It was time, but it was too simple. There must be something that he was forgetting. He walked to the window. The sun had reached the top of the barn door and his mind raced in search of options. It hurt to swallow and his arms felt weak and lifeless. He thought he could hear the dull rhythm of his heart, his eardrums expanding and contracting with its cadence.

The cornfield that bordered the barnyard was dark in the foreground, a jungle of leaves not yet touched by the sun. He stared at the dark border, unable to take his eyes from the black wall of waving leaves. His head pounded as the rhythm resonated louder, a deep bass that made him feel sick to his stomach.

The runner appeared from the darkness of the corn, his flight suit indistinguishable in color from the background. In slow motion, he slipped as he rounded the corner of the barn, his hand touching the ground; he righted himself and kept running. Clods of Laotion mud flew from the soles of his boots. He ran for his life. With fearful determination he ran straight toward Eden, his eyes locked on Eden's, his mouth gasping for air, arms pumping with clenched fists. Yellow-orange muzzle flashes blinked from the dark field behind him. Eden could hear the shrill whine of the turbo-jet engine above the low-toned cadence of the main rotor. Above the din he could hear a voice in the background, garbled, slow, and repetitive in its one-word order. Eden knew what the order was, but his limbs were unresponsive. He could only focus on the face of the runner. The runner reached out with one arm, prematurely; a gesture appealing for help, begging for seconds. He ran with everything left in him, but gained nothing. Instead he became smaller, shrinking as Eden rose above him. In the background the garbled order was sluggishly persistent, "Fire, fire, fire."

CHAPTER 11

"And the poor dead, when they have left the walled
And silvery city of the now hopeless body
Where are they to go, Oh where are they to go?"
D. H. Lawrence
"All Souls Day"

1971

THE WALKING DEAD WERE ALL AROUND HIM. They were casualties of war, even without being killed or wounded. Their wounds were sometimes dressed with cowardice, sometimes bravado. Some attempted to heal themselves with drugs or alcohol, which made them stoned and happy, drunk and depressed. Some took refuge with the bar girls and whores of the boom-boom houses, finding their comfort with flat-chested teenage girls who listened without understanding. Men of war were weak, with all the human frailties lurking just below the artificial threshold created by booze or Buddha grass. Three months of monsoon only made them weaker.

Eden had waited weeks for a chance to call home, his name and time calendared since early November. His three-minute opportunity to escape the realities of war was scheduled for 0200 hours. The surprise call would catch his parents at lunch the day before, a time religiously adhered to on the ranch. Eden did not understand the complexities of the call that involved satellites, HAM radio operators, and ground lines. His father seemed confused by the process and had little to say. He could not remember to say "over," at the end of his short statements and had difficulty hearing Eden. The HAM operator in Missoula had to repeat Eden's comments to him. The sound of his father's voice caused Eden's throat to narrow, a stricture that held back the explosive emotions building within his chest.

"Thirty seconds," the radio operator warned.

"Tell Mom hi," Eden said.

"What?"

"He said to tell his mother hello," the Montanan repeated.

"She's down to Saratoga gettin' her hair done."

"I love you, Pop."

"What?"

"He says he loves you."

"What'd he say? I can't hear him."

"I'm sorry, your time is up," said the COMSAT operator in Saigon. He thanked the HAM operator in Missoula and told Eden to hang up. The clerk at the crew dispatch headquarters where the call was received had given Eden privacy. He stood outside smoking. Eden bummed a smoke, thanked him for the phone, and walked across the tarmac toward Dead Man's Barn. He had barely entered the dark corridor between the pallets of aluminum caskets when the stricture in his throat suddenly opened. His loneliness and fear escaped in raspy surges, his eyes burned with tears.

*****

Eden's short-timer calendar took on color. With conviction he pulled it from his footlocker every night to color another square further up the maiden's leg. The paper was frayed and smudged with water stains. It had rained almost continuously for more than a hundred days. Flying had been cold and treacherous. Ceilings were so low that they were forced to find their way back to Da Nang by following rivers and coastlines, often only fifty feet above the ground. They spent much of their time ferrying spooks and brass between ground units.

They had lost their entire sister crew and a brigadier general in early December. Rough Rider had flown him out into the Gulf of Tonkin and put down on the fantail of the USS Brisbane. Upon liftoff, amid heavy seas, they had caught the landing gear on a cable guardrail and pitched into the ocean. Mike Delaney, the starboard door gunner, had not yet hooked his harness and had fallen headlong into the main rotor just before hitting the water. They'd recovered Mike's lower torso, his tags laced neatly in his boots. The four crew members were never mentioned, but the brigadier general made *The Stars and Stripes* as the highest ranking American officer to be lost in the Vietnam conflict.

Eden had stripped Mike's bed and turned in his sheets to the quartermaster. Mike had bunked in Little Nail's stall. He had found two Baby Ruth candy bar wrappers stuffed under Mike Delaney's mattress. They smelled of chocolate. Mike had received a care package from home earlier in the week. To avoid the bum's rush by hungry chopper crews, he had enjoyed his bounty in the privacy of his darkened hooch. Eden thought it ironic that in return for a cardboard box of broken cookies, candy, and the artwork of a little brother, Mike's parents would receive an aluminum box with the remains of half of their son. Later that night, Eden had stared at his short-timer's calendar, divided the remaining days by seven, then struck a match to its corner. He did not want his parents to be embarrassed when they received the manila envelope containing his personal possessions; his aluminum box would be traumatic enough.

*****

"Cowboy?"

"Yeah."

"It's Goose. What the hell? Over."

"Hi, Ivan. Good to hear from you. How they hanging?" Eden said into the phone at dispatch HQ.

"Better now," Ivan said. "Got me a terrible dose in Da Nang last month. Thank God for penicillin."

"Sorry to hear that, but you ought not to go weenie dippin' in those nasty whorehouses."

"Easy for you to say, you faggot," Ivan said. "How long's it been since you took Mr. Wiggly out for a little exercise?"

"Mr. Wiggly?"

"You know, your Wyoming sheep poker."

Eden smiled. "What's up, Goose?"

"Waterskiing."

"Waterskiing?"

"I've got a friend across the river who borrowed a boat from the Navy, a seventeen-foot aluminum job with a ninety-horse Johnson on it. He somehow got skis and a towrope. What do you say?"

"I say you're nuts," Eden said, without hesitation.

"The Old Man is off to Bangkok for a conjugal visit with his missus. We're heading downriver in the morning. When we get to the gulf we'll shoot up the coast to Monkey Mountain. I hear there's a great beach there. Can you get off? Are you on standby?"

"You tell me. You're the one that keeps sending us all over Southeast Asia at all hours of the day and night," Eden said.

He stared at a series of pictures under the Plexiglas pad on the dispatch clerk's desk. They were all the same naked young woman in various pornographic poses. He pointed to one of the most obscene and raised his eyebrows at the clerk, who reclined behind the desk, bored, his hands clasped behind his head.

"My wife," the clerk said.

Eden gave him the thumbs-up sign and turned away. "We just came in from Quang Tri. I should be all right."

"Outstanding!" Ivan shouted.

"What about sharks?" Eden said.

"Don't fall."

"I've never water skied before."

"Don't be a pussy, Cowboy."

* * * * *

The South China Sea was rough, swallowing the small boat between swells, sometimes lifting the stern and propeller out of the water. The boat's motor raced intermittently. Ivan steered with a broad smile pasted on his face. The boat thief and his friend, neither of whom Eden had ever met, sat in the bow, puking over the gunwales. The day was beautiful, one of the first sunny days in months. The sea was the color of light jade along the coast, a translucent band of frothy green between the dark blue of horizonless ocean and the white foam of waves breaking on sandy beaches. The sea was much calmer further out in dark water, but Ivan piloted the boat at open throttle along the jade interface between shallow and deep. He was looking for something.

"Thar she blows!" Ivan yelled, pointing toward shore.

The long, sandy beach swept upward into steep jungle-covered hills. Tucked between two verdant mounts, a crystalline waterfall plummeted over a moss-covered bluff into a small pool at the top of the beach.

"Holy shit!" the boat thief yelled, then followed with a war hoop.

Ivan landed the boat and the four of them hauled it high on the beach. Goose ran toward the base of the cliff, clothes flying above his head. A trail of jungle fatigues, boots, and olive drab underwear marked the four men's route to the waterfall. The pool was deep with no above-ground outlet. Ivan led the ascent over jagged rocks and slippery moss. The four white men, naked and single file, inched their way along the waterfall's edge to the top of the cliff. Eden believed black men looked better naked than white guys. Outdoors, white boys always had a freshly skinned appearance.

Standing shoulder-to-shoulder, they peered over the edge at the tiny pool beneath them. Like the ocean, the pool's edge was a light green color; its center appeared black.

"No way," the boat thief's friend finally said.

"You're fucking nuts, Goose," said the boat thief.

Eden knew that was all Ivan needed to send him over the edge.

"Grab your balls before you hit the water, boys. At this height, they'll get ripped off," Ivan said, taking a step backward. Launching himself over the edge he fell silently toward the pool. Legs together, he was vertical with the world. He brought his hands to his genitals just before breaking the surface in front of the white aeration of the waterfall. He disappeared with minimal splash and sound. He surfaced quickly and yelled his approval and encouragement. One by one they followed, leaping from the cliff and falling toward the miniature pool. The slightest miscalculation would have sent them to a rock hard death. Again and again they scaled the slippery cliff, laughing with delight as they defied death.

"Would you do this back in Seattle, Goose?" Eden asked as they looked over the edge, the stream tugging at their ankles.

"Only if I was trying to kill myself." He paused then looked at Eden. "How about you?"

"Hell, I don't even know how to swim."

Ivan did not respond. He looked at Eden and smiled his understanding. They locked elbows and leapt from the cliff together.

The four of them laid in a row in the white sand of the beach. They had put on their olive drab boxers to keep their privates from getting sunburned. Ivan and his friends smoked long, pre-packaged joints they claimed were laced with something special. Eden preferred to smoke cigarettes. They had brought nothing to eat or drink. The drugs made Ivan and his friends giddy as they swapped the typical GI yarns of sexual conquest, physical superiority, and mental genius. Occasionally, they would turn toward Eden and bleat like sheep, then begin another story that always started with, "I once met this chick . . . ." Eden joined in with a story that began, "I once knew this sheep, her name was Ewela." The group howled with delight, especially when Eden told of looking into the gold of her horizontal irises, the sweet smell of alfalfa on her breath.

The low rumble of a diesel engine silenced them. Standing, they saw a grey Navy LST plowing through the surf toward the beach. No one spoke.

The large, rectangular steel box, sounding like a bulldozer, hit the beach in front of the four soldiers who stood in their underwear, mouths agape. The hydraulic landing ramp quickly lowered to the sandy beach with a thump. A cheer from within the craft arose as a half dozen sailors raced down the ramp to the beach, led by several young Vietnamese women who were totally naked. Two gobs bringing up the rear carried a half oil drum barbecue grill and a huge ice chest. They appeared to be regular Navy, dressed in denim dungarees and light blue work shirts, their white Navy caps cocked on the backs of their heads. Eden noticed they all wore low-cut, black oxford shoes.

The women screeched as men chased them into the ocean. Catching them, they would swing them by their hands and feet, counting in exaggerated fashion to three and releasing them into the frothy surf. Two of the women, laughing with delight, tried to escape their tormentors by circling the four soldiers, keeping the Army between themselves and the Navy in a game of cat and mouse.

"*Choi oie. Choi duc oie.* You numbah ten GI, you boo-coo *dien cai dau!*" a women shouted toward the sailors as she raced behind Ivan and Eden. She appeared to be the oldest, late twenties perhaps, with firm, pointy breasts.

"Ten hut," Ivan barked with authority.

Eden looked at him, puzzled. The gobs suddenly stopped and the women quieted.

"Who the hell is in charge here?" Ivan commanded.

A short, stocky sailor with heavy black beard stubble and thick eyebrows said, "No one, Sir."

"Report," Ivan barked.

"Third Class Petty Officer Cozzilino, Boatswain's Mate, U.S.S. Delaware, Sir."

Ivan leaned to look around the sailor at the LST. "Is that your landing craft, Sailor?"

"Yes Sir, I mean no, Sir."

"Yes or no, for Christ's sake."

"No, Sir."

"Whose is it?"

"The U.S. Navy's, Sir."

Ivan looked at him suspiciously. "You getting smart with me, Cozzilino?"

"No, Sir."

"Did you steal that LST?"

"Just borrowed it, Sir."

Ivan paused and looked slowly from sailor to sailor, who all looked ready to bolt. "Who are these women?" he said.

"Whores, Sir," Cozzilino said without hesitation.

"Are they here of their own free will?"

"We paid them, Sir."

"Why are you on my beach?" Ivan said, leaning forward, looking directly into the sailor's eyes.

Cozzilino looked away. "Shore leave, Sir. We're all on shore leave to China Beach at Da Nang."

"Does this look like fucking China Beach, you dickhead?"

"No, Sir."

"What's in that ice chest?"

"Beer and steaks."

"Steaks?"

"T-bones," Cozzilino said. He nodded at the sailor standing next to the large chest. The sailor opened the lid and pulled out a large, thick, red T-bone and held it up for Ivan to see.

"Did you steal those, too?" Ivan said.

"We borrowed them, Sir, from the officer's mess. We have plenty, Sir. We'd be pleased to share with you and your men."

"Now you're talking, sailor," Ivan said with a devilish smile. "And why do you keep calling me 'sir'?"

Cozzilino looked at Ivan for a long moment, then to the other soldiers. "You're not an officer?"

"Nope."

The sailor looked to his friends who all stood motionless. He pushed his hat back on his head revealing a thick, black crew cut. "You mean this is all bullshit?"

"Absolutely."

"You been jacking us around?"

"Uh huh," Ivan said, now smiling broadly.

"What the fuck for?"

"For fun, you dumb Dago."

Cozzilino's eyes doubled in size. "Who you callin' a Dago?"

"You, you stupid Guinea. I'll speak slower. I forgot I was talking to the U.S. Navy." Ivan turned toward Eden and said, "What a bunch of thieving faggots."

Cozzilino's first punch caught Ivan under his right ear. Ivan staggered backward, sending a whore to all fours. There was an awkward moment of silence and motionless staring. Then the gobs rushed the four of them in unison, charging head-down. Sand and punches flew in the ensuing brawl. The Army was outnumbered by nearly two to one, but made a respectable showing. The whores screeched and jabbered; one jumped on Ivan's back and he continued to fight. The woman rode him, twirling and bucking. A second whore mounted Cozzilino and began pulling and tugging at the woman atop Ivan. Within moments all four whores had climbed onto the shoulders of the combatants. Someone yelled, "Chicken fight!" and the swirling mass moved into the surf. No one seemed concerned with the bloody noses, split lips, or swollen eyes. The event had turned into athletic competition: naked women astraddle the necks of men, attempting to dismount each other.

They laughed until they were hoarse. Even the whores seemed to enjoy their day at the beach. The Navy shared their beer and steaks. The men sat, intermingled, talking quietly and cutting their steaks with borrowed silverware on borrowed white china plates that they held in their laps. The women squatted in a circle, mamasan style. They passed steaks between them, ripping and tearing at the meat like wild dogs, then laughing. A seaman from Nashville drawled, "How come them women don't have hair on their pussies?"

There was silence as everyone thought of a smart answer, then laughter at the realization that they did not have one.

Ivan and his friends shared their Buddha grass and a pile of empty Budweiser cans grew steadily. Ivan, Cozzilino, and one of the women scaled the cliff and with much taunting and theatrics, fell into the pool below.

The darkness of war seemed distant. Eden, for the moment, forgot about Mike Delaney and the other casualties of America's misguided effort. Only the moment seemed to matter. When he closed his eyes with the warmth of the sun on his body, the sound of waves breaking against the beach, and laughter in the background, he imagined he was, again, on spring break at South Padre Island. Vietnam did not exist during spring break. It was somebody else's war, eight thousand miles away. Eden wished that when he opened his eyes he would see his fraternity brothers, beers in hand, hovering over round-eyed, bikini-clad coeds with light-colored hair. He kept his eyes closed.

Dark clouds gathered over the top of Monkey Mountain and the temperature cooled with the return of the late season monsoon. The NVA sniper shifted the crosshairs to each of the four men who stood at attention in their shorts, saluting the men in the landing craft as it pulled from the beach and headed for open water. Perspiration beaded across his forehead as he watched the Americans gather their clothes.

* * * * *

It was dark and raining steadily when Ivan cut to half throttle and turned the boat toward the dock on the Da Nang side of the river. Eden sat in the bow looking back over the dark water. The two dead soldiers lay in the bottom of the boat.

CHAPTER 12

"In the little town the news ran quickly.
It was communicated by whispers in doorways,
by quick, meaningful looks."
John Steinbeck
The Moon Is Down

1975

HAPPY NEW YEAR, EDEN," ELIZABETH SAID. She wore a white, loose-knit stocking cap with a large pom-pom on top. Her cheeks were pink with cold.

"Happy New Year to you, too," Eden said, his voice faltering. "I'm surprised to see you. I haven't seen you in town lately. Of course, I've been gone. Went home for the holidays. Wyoming. Did you have a good Christmas? Where's Jessica? How's your dad?"

"Take a breath, Eden. Are you going to invite me in?"

Her sparkling eyes and broad smile held his gaze. For a moment, he was uncertain if his voice would return. He looked over his shoulder at the basement apartment. It was clean and orderly to a fault. Still, he was embarrassed by his meager surroundings. "Of course. I'm sorry. Come in."

"Reminds me of college," she said, looking around the room.

"How so?"

"I think I lived in half the basements in Ames."

"Funny, I had you figured for a sorority girl living in a brick house with Greek letters on the front."

"I was a Pi Phi, but only because my mother was," she said, pulling off her stocking cap.

"Your mother went to college?" he asked, a little too quickly.

"Yes. Why do you find that strange?"

"Oh, I don't. I just thought . . . since Carl doesn't . . . . How'd your folks meet?"

"Mom was one of the Schaeffer clan. She grew up just a few miles down the road. They went all through school together, but never dated until they were in college."

"Your dad went to college?" he said, again much too quickly.

"Don't be fooled by his sarcasm toward college graduates. He was an AGR who graduated with honors in agronomy with a minor in soil science."

"I was an AGR," Eden said. "I don't get it. He's always poking at me for being a college boy. Why does he always ask me questions about plant science and production methods? He's an agronomist for crying out loud."

"He likes you. It's just his way. Do you mind if I take my coat off?"

"Please," he said, taking her coat and cap. He smelled the sweet musk of her perfume. "How about a cup of coffee? Have you had breakfast yet?"

"I'd love a cup of tea if you have some. We had breakfast hours ago."

"Earl Grey okay?"

"My favorite."

"Where's Jessica?"

"Dad took her with him to Burlington. He had a doctor's appointment and then was going to visit his sister. Aunt Gretchen loves to see Jessica. She also loves to stuff her full of cookies and candy and spoil her."

"What brings you to town on a Saturday morning?" he called from the kitchen area next to the furnace.

"I came to see you, Eden." She slowly toured the one-room apartment. She cocked her head to read the titles of the books on the makeshift cinderblock shelves. She was surprised to see Willa Cather and Edna Ferber next to London and Hemingway. Joseph Conrad, Sinclair Lewis, and William Faulkner were well represented. She had expected to see Will James and Zane Grey.

Eden did not respond. He busied himself in the kitchen area, his back to the living room. A few minutes of strained silence passed before he entered the room, carrying a coffee mug and a saucer with several lemon cream cookies. "Sorry about the teacup. Do you take cream or sugar?"

"A little sugar if you have it."

He returned with his cup and a box of sugar cubes. Elizabeth sat in the worn, overstuffed chair—the only chair—and Eden sat on the edge of the bed. They shared the wobbly end table next to the floor lamp.

"What about?" he finally said, as if their earlier conversation had continued uninterrupted.

"I want to explain about the other night."

"The other night?"

"Thanksgiving."

"That was more than a month ago. And no explanation is necessary. Cookie?" he asked, offering the lemon creams.

"No thanks. And yes, I need to explain," she said, circling the rim of her coffee mug with her finger. "I don't expect you to understand, because I don't even know what happened."

Eden looked down. "First, you shouldn't have such low expectations of my ability to comprehend. Second, I really don't want to hear you explain away what happened as a fluke, or some terrible mistake, when it's something *I've* thought about every day for the past month. Something that was . . ." he paused and looked down. "Good," he said softly.

Elizabeth sipped her tea, pushed her hair back, and leaned forward. "I've thought about it every day, too, Eden. And yes, it was very good."

The ceiling creaked loudly and dust particles danced within the beam of sunlight that shone through the basement window, a yellow shaft angling to the floor separating them.

"Mrs. Nagy, my landlady. She's fat," Eden said.

"I know. She was fat when I was a little girl. She worked in the grade school cafeteria."

They looked at each other and smiled. Eden noticed how soft she appeared on the other side of the sunbeam.

"Eden, my husband has been gone for three years."

"You don't have to tell me this."

"I want to tell you. I need to tell you." She leaned back in the chair and looked away. "We met in college. He was two years ahead of me. We were married a month after I graduated. We moved to California and I got pregnant with Jessica a few months later." She paused and turned toward Eden. "Isn't it amazing how you can condense years of your life into a few sentences?"

Eden only blinked in recognition of her question.

"Don't get me wrong. It wasn't one of those slam, bam, thank you ma'am relationships. It was the stuff fairy tales are made of. Life was very, very good."

They heard the front door of the house above close.

"Even my dad liked him and that was a rare occurrence. He disliked every guy I ever dated. He likes you, you know."

Eden smiled slightly.

"In case you hadn't noticed, he's been trying to play the role of matchmaker with us."

"Really? I thought he liked me for my chess skills and knowledge of modern farming practices," he said sarcastically.

"You'd have spent Christmas at our house if he could have found you. Around the house his hints aren't very subtle. Yesterday he said, 'Why don't you call Eden and ask him out for dinner?'" she said in a low voice. "'Dinner,' I said, 'why stop there? Why don't I take him to Acapulco or a cheap motel in Vegas and then to the nearest wedding chapel? That's what you really want, isn't it Dad?' I said."

Eden looked embarrassed. "What is it that you really want?" he said, looking directly at her.

She looked away, her eyes glassy with tears. She turned toward him and was about to speak when someone knocked loudly on the apartment door.

Eden opened the door; Mrs. Nagy stood there panting from the exertion of walking down the stairs.

"Sorry to bother you, Eden." Her voice was irritatingly scratchy. "But that old furnace is acting up again. I thought I better check on it," she said, pushing past him. "Oh dear, I am doubly sorry. I didn't know you had company," she said, looking at Elizabeth.

Eden stood behind her and rolled his eyes. He knew she had been watching and listening. She would telegraph the Keotonka Rumormonger Club after circling the furnace once.

"Hi, Mrs. Nagy. It's Elizabeth Peterson. It's nice to see you."

"Oh my, Elizabeth, I haven't seen you in ages. I don't get out much anymore. My legs are just no good. My diabetes is just off the chart lately. The doctor says I need to lose some weight. You're absolutely skinny, dear. How's Carl?" She still gulped for air.

"He's fine. He never knows what to do with himself in January. Heaven forbid that he take a vacation."

"Did I ever tell you that I had a huge crush on Carl when we were in middle school?" Mrs. Nagy said.

Eden thought that *huge* was the operative word in her question.

Elizabeth smiled politely.

"Well, let's have a look at that furnace," she said, lumbering toward the dark half of the basement. She circled it once, clanging something on the far side. "Let's hope that does it. I can't afford a repairman. I'm on a fixed income, you know, and the prices of prescriptions are just outrageous." She headed for the door. "It was nice to see you again, dear," she said smiling at Elizabeth. "You really should come by sometime and see my scrapbook. I kept news clippings about all the children I worked with over the years."

"I'll do that sometime," Elizabeth said. She tried to be enthusiastic.

Mrs. Nagy stopped at the doorway and turned toward her. "I have the clippings of your wedding in that book, dear. My, what a handsome couple you were. Give my best to your father," she said, and disappeared out the door.

Closing the door behind her, Eden shook his head, bristling with anger. "She knew full well you were here," he whispered.

Elizabeth said, "I should be going." She looked for her coat and cap. "This town . . . ," She paused and shook her head. "It's been three years."

"Please don't go," he said, walking toward her.

She turned away from him and stood facing the window. "Why did you come here, Eden?" she asked without turning around. "Everything was fine until you showed up."

"Do you want me to leave?" he said. "If you tell me to leave, I'll pack up and be gone by noon and you'll never see me again. Tell me if that's what you want me to do."

She continued to face away from him. Slowly, with lowered head, she turned. She raised her face to look at him; tears streaked her cheeks. "Yes, I want you to leave," she said softly, her lower lip quivering. She carefully wiped the tears from her face with each hand then said, "But please don't." She took a step toward him and he met her halfway.

He had meant only to embrace her, to comfort her, to let her know that he understood. But they found each other's lips and kissed fully. He pulled her tightly against him. He could feel the softness of her breasts and the slight protuberance of her lower stomach against his body. Her perfume made him hungry for her, ravenous to consume her. He wanted to immerse himself in the taste and feel of her. He felt himself slipping away, succumbing to a dreamlike fogginess that warmly enveloped him.

"Eden," she whispered. "There is so much I need to tell you."

"No," he whispered back. "Whatever you have to say is history. It can't be changed. It's today and tomorrow that counts. I can't look back anymore. The past haunts me every day and at night in my dreams. I'm afraid that someday I'll get trapped back there and I'll never see you again. The past has nothing good for me. I don't want to talk about it or even think about it."

She responded by again finding his lips. He had never experienced passion with such intensity. He returned it without effort.

*****

Eden heated a can of soup for lunch. They sat sipping apple juice and nibbling on saltines. They ate silently, occasionally looking at each other and smiling. Elizabeth's blouse was buttoned unevenly and neither of them had bothered with shoes or socks. Their feet flirted intimately in a game of footsie under the tiny kitchen table. Still, they did not speak.

After lunch Eden walked to the basement window and looked out. "There's quite a crowd gathered in the street. Looks like Mrs. Nagy is giving an interview to the press."

Grinning broadly, Elizabeth gently pushed in front of him. Rising on her toes she reached for the window's ledge to look out. Her blouse rose, exposing a band of flesh across her lower back. Pulling her hair aside, he kissed her on the side of the neck. She closed her eyes.

The short, winter day grew dusky. The ceiling creaked and they both stared upward.

"I need to go," she said. "Dad and Jessica will be home in less than an hour."

"Will you come back?"

"Eden, I've been here for seven hours. Take a breath."

"I mean tomorrow, next week, next year," he said.

She stared at him, her eyes searching his. He was afraid of what her answer would be. Yes or no would be equally devastating. "Don't answer that," he said suddenly, and placed his fingers against her lips.

"Maybe," she whispered.

"I can live with maybe," he said, and kissed her.

*****

The night air was painfully cold. His nostrils burned each time he inhaled and his skin felt tight across his face. The smoky odor of fried food hung in the still air outside the restaurant. He was hungry but did not feel like eating alone. With hunched shoulders and hands thrust deep into his coat pockets, he walked to the river. Beyond the borders of ice, the open channel appeared black. Black and cold like the Iowa night that surrounded him. Inhaling deeply, his chest convulsed involuntarily with emotion. It had been building since the door had closed behind her. He had fought to repress it, but knew that battle would be lost. The form it would take would always surprise him. Sometimes he cried, sometimes he cussed. The worst was when it settled over him with a heavy dampness, wrapping around his shoulders and over his head. He turned and looked back toward Main Street, hoping that something would distract him and stall the dank shroud from descending over him. He loved her. It was not his intention.

CHAPTER 13

"To do good to mankind is the chivalrous plan,
And is always as nobly requited;
Then battle for freedom wherever you can,
And, if not shot or hang'd, you'll get knighted."
Lord Byron
"Stanzas"

1971

AT 20,000 FEET VIETNAM APPEARED AT PEACE, EVEN pastoral. The T-39 Learjet seemed spacious inside as it reduced the time from Da Nang to Saigon to a mere hour. Eden was nervous, not just because he was the only passenger, but because he had been summoned. Transporting an E-5 door gunner by jet was intimidating, especially when he did not know the purpose.

At Tan Son Nhut, a shiny, black Ford pulled onto the tarmac before the Lear rolled to a stop. The driver was a captain in crisp khakis who placed Eden in the backseat without a word. He drove cautiously through the crowded streets of Saigon. The motor scooters and three-wheeled rickshaws choked the streets with colorful confusion amid the powder blue haze of exhaust fumes. The captain's West Point ring, prominent on his right hand, shone from atop the steering wheel. Eden could smell the man's Bay Rum aftershave and he noted the close-cropped hair and shaved hairlines on his pocked neck. The Westy had been a teenager with acne. Now he was a mannequin with a rod up his ass and bars on his shoulders. He never spoke to Eden.

Somewhere in the middle of the city among large white, colonial-style buildings, the sedan pulled up to a forbidding iron gate topped with concertina wire. An MP scrutinized the occupants, saluted, and opened the gate. At the side of the building the captain nosed the car into a narrow, steep incline that disappeared under the columned building. At the bottom he reached from the window to a keypad and punched in a code that raised a large metal, roll-up door and the car continued its descent into the underground blackness. A door appeared in the headlights and the sedan stopped. Another captain appeared and opened the car door for Eden. He placed a small chain over Eden's head and around his neck. From the chain a large, pink, laminated plastic tag dangled with the number *seven* embossed in black. Eden was reminded of the whores he had seen in Bangkok who wore similar chains with numbers and danced with each other on a strobe-lighted dance floor.

No words were spoken, no orders given, as Eden followed behind the officer who led him down a series of concrete corridors and flights of stairs, and through electronically locked and coded doors. He was shown into a very dark room and the door closed behind him. Lights slowly illuminated a small theater complete with red velvet theater seats. A screen lowered from the ceiling and a beam of light flashed from the projection booth at the back of the darkened room. Eden was shown an hour-long propaganda film about SOG's history and mission and the evils of the North Vietnamese Communists. The film described, in simplistic fashion, the use of the McQuire Rigs and Fulton Recovery Systems for extracting downed pilots, commando units, and counterinsurgents; various code-named SOG offensives; and the roles of the three SOG

Command Centers and their Forward Operating Bases. At the film's conclusion, the lights came on; Captain Number Two entered and escorted Eden to a small room furnished with a rectangular table and a single chair on each side.

A full bird colonel entered, carrying a large three-ring binder. Eden rose to attention.

"At ease, Cain. Be seated."

Eden tried to read the shiny bronze name tag above his right pocket, but could not make it out. The colonel sat, folded his hands and looked at Eden. The officer bore an amazing resemblance to Woody Woodpecker, he thought. His red hair had turned light with age, but his sharp facial features and large eyes gave him a surprised look.

"You're a real fuckup, aren't you Cain?" the Colonel said. The crows feet that radiated back from each eye toward silvery-orange temples were exaggerated by his harsh squint.

"Sir?"

"You're not one of us, Sergeant. You'll never be one of us. You're a goddamned, pansy-assed, no nuts, fuckoff door gunner who just happens to be SOG cleared. Do you even know what SOG stands for?"

"Studies and Observations Group, formerly Special Operations Group, Sir," Eden said.

"No, you little pussy. Do you know what SOG stands for? Who we are, what we do, and why we do it?"

Eden now knew the question was rhetorical and did not attempt to answer.

"Well, let me tell you what it stands for, soldier. It stands for the best goddamned fighting machine in the history of warfare. It stands for freedom and democracy. It stands for personal sacrifice. It stands for guts and balls, the likes of which you'll never understand. SOG stands for winning. It stands for the most formidable assault force ever assembled.

It stands for a group of secret warriors that will never see the medals or the recognition they deserve. Hell, many of them will never receive a funeral or have their remains united with family. Heroes that don't exist," he added, his voice trailing off.

Eden stared at him, trying not to show his fear. He knew what SOG was. He had gone through the indoctrination program in the underground bunkers of Command and Control North at XXIV Corps shortly after arriving in country. They had started the background checks on him before he left stateside. His clearances were as high as they get: TS, SI, SOG. Top Secret, Special Intelligence, Studies and Observations Group.

"There isn't a thing we don't know about you, Sergeant Cain," the Colonel said, opening the large binder. "From that little cowgirl, Jody Parker, you were humping in high school, to the C-minus you got on your Physics midterm your senior year at U.W." He looked up to see if he had Eden's attention. He had. He flipped through the pages of the notebook, a slight grin on his face. "Last month your mother got a brown rinse at Cathy's Cut and Curl in Saratoga to cover the gray on her German-Irish head. Your father ordered a rebuilt generator for that old John Deere MC crawler tractor from a parts company in Wichita, Kansas. He's using that beat-up old relic to plow feed lanes for his cattle since snowpack in the mountains around Encampment is 130 percent of normal this winter." He looked up again to determine Eden's response. "Did your old man ever tell you about the time he got tossed in the slammer in Rawlins for beating the shit out of some cowboy in a bar? It was August, 1939."

Eden raised his eyebrows slightly. His father was the most gentle, even-tempered man he had ever known.

"Do you know about your older sister?"

Eden wanted to speak now. He did not have a sister and he felt the anger rising in him.

"She was born deader than a mackerel in 1945, six months after your parents were married. Did you know her name, Sergeant?"

"Your point, Sir?" Eden asked through clenched teeth.

"Did you know her name?" he shouted.

Eden said nothing.

"Baby Girl," he said with a smirk on his face. "Baby Girl is all it said on the death certificate. What the hell kind of parents would bury their daughter without a name?" He waited for Eden to respond without taking his eyes off him. "The same kind of parents that would raise a dumb shit, inbred retard like you."

The muscles in Eden's jaw rippled, but he said nothing.

"Did you think we let you out of our sight for a minute when you took your R&R in Hawaii? When all your buddies were pounding the pork to the whores in Singapore, you—Mr. High and Mighty, Clean Living—took your R&R in Hawaii, where all the married men go to meet their wives. Just wanted some round-eyed nookie, didn't you? Just think what you could have gotten with that same forty bucks in Singapore." He smiled at Eden.

"And what about that weekend mission in Thailand? Got to thinking about that nasty snatch when you got back to Da Nang, didn't you, Sergeant? You went to see the pecker checker a week later. That cotton swab up the old pisser hurts, doesn't it?" He smiled again. "And that dumb shit stunt you pulled on Monkey Mountain cost two boys their lives. What the hell were you thinking? You are not to venture into unsecured areas with your clearances. We should have sent your ass to the brig." He paused and rubbed his hands together in a washing motion. "The point, Sergeant Cain, is that we know everything about you, your family, your friends, your dirty little secrets, even things you don't know. Things you don't want to know."

Eden stared soberly at him.

"Sergeant, your record would appear to regular Army as being impressive. To SOG it means nothing. You're no swinging dick hero. We don't recognize valor. We don't recognize our wounded or our dead. What we recognize is trust. Our existence depends upon loyalty. We tolerated your Monkey Mountain escapade because you've been a good soldier, a brave soldier, and we know you're not Special Forces, not one of us. But by damn, you are SOG cleared and attached to a SOG unit, and you fly SOG missions, and I will not tolerate your disloyalty to us. Do I make myself clear?"

"No, Sir," Eden said.

"You best not be jacking me, boy. I'll take you upstairs and put a bullet in your head myself." He rose out of his chair and leaned over the table, neck bulging, woodpecker nose reddening, fists clenched. "You don't question our missions, Sergeant. You don't nose around in military records. You don't concern yourself with where you are going, where you've been, or what you did when you got there. You keep your filthy stink hole shut. Your job is to carry out orders and once that's done, to wait for the next order. Don't you ever second-guess our mission, Mister. Don't you ever go off on your own asking questions about what we do. I'll have you in Corrective Custody so fast with a truckload of shit for charges that you'll be eating soft food and pissing in your pants before you get out of this man's army. Everyone you have talked to since your last Bright Light is gone. Your buddy, Specialist Karnow, is filing motor pool parts requests with the Eighth Army in Japan and that's only because General Wellborn intervened. Airman Good with Da Nang Tactical Air Command got his black ass run over by a forklift and is recovering nicely in Manila. That little blonde Red Cross Donut Dolly with the big tits that promised to help you has her own crisis to deal with. Seems she was raped and traumatized, hasn't said a word to anyone since she arrived stateside."

Eden felt nauseous, light-headed, and starved for oxygen. He wanted to run from the room, swim to the surface, and gulp air in the bright of day.

"Did you think we would ignore your disloyalty just because you're a short-timer?" the Colonel said, sitting again. "We've got your number, Cain. We'll be watching you like a lizard watches a fly. If you so much as wipe your ass with your left hand, we'll lose your paperwork and you'll be in this man's army until the lead falls out of your pencil. Do I make myself clear now, Sergeant?"

"Yes, Sir."

"And don't think this will end if, by chance, you muster out. The privilege of serving with SOG guarantees you a lifetime of watchful protection. You don't ever have to worry about the Commies torturing you for information because we'll get to you first. When and if you debrief, soldier, you'll sign the rest of your life away. SOG doesn't exist. Our missions never happened. If you so much as mention SOG while in a drunken stupor at a cocktail party, we'll take you out. How will we know? The hippie with the ponytail, the chick in the tight dress, the geezer with hair in his ears will be ours. We'll watch you, we'll test you. You fuck up, we'll kill you. Am I now making myself clear, Mister?"

"Yes, Sir."

"Don't disappoint me, soldier."

"No, Sir."

The Colonel arose and left the room. Escorts reappeared and the trip back to Da Nang was undertaken in reverse order of the trip to Saigon. Eden did not remember the color and chaos of Saigon streets on the return trip. He remembered very little of the flight back. Their mission had been to scare him and it had worked. He sat by himself at the mess hall that evening. His hand shook uncontrollably, food spilled from his fork.

The mosquito netting was tucked tightly around the edges of his mattress. In the dark he felt secure. He was exhausted but knew he could not sleep. There was much to think about. He started with Ivan and imagined him in gray surroundings someplace in Japan. The Goose could take care of himself. He would make the best of a bad situation and have fun doing it. He saw him walking down a street, laughing, a kimono-clad woman on each arm. Ivan had told him nothing he did not already know.

Airman Good was as innocent as they came. He was conscientious and sincere. Eden could not remember ever talking with a black man before entering the Army. Louis Good from Mississippi fascinated Eden with his Southern drawl. Eden was unsure if he had lied to Louis to get the information he wanted. Louis was trusting and had given it to him without question.

Shelly Robinson was innocent, too, but in a more naïve way. She had appeared at headquarters one day in her light blue Red Cross dress, handing out donated paperback books. Soldiers crowded around her to see and talk with a white woman. They hadn't been interested in her books, although some took a book or two in an attempt to be polite. They'd been interested in her large breasts, white skin, round eyes, and blonde hair. Eden had waited at the end of the line to get a book and a glimpse of her bra between strained buttonholes. When he'd asked what she recommended, she'd dug through the box of books and handed him *The French Lieutenant's Woman* and the *The Summer of '42.*

Two weeks later she had returned with more paperbacks and surprised him when she'd asked if he had enjoyed the two books, recalling them by title. They'd sat on the steps of headquarters for more than an hour, smoking and discussing John Fowles's Sarah Woodruff and Herman Raucher's delicately humorous description of Hermie's love affair with the older, married Dorothy. Shelly was from the Upper Peninsula of Michigan and wealthy, pretty, and idealistic. She had dropped out of Smith in order to make her contribution to the war she detested. The same GIs had walked by several times, tilting their heads as they'd looked up her dress. She'd seemed unaffected by their attention and quipped that she was glad she had worn clean panties. Shelly had promised, without question, to check on what he requested of her. He never saw her again.

That night his dreams were fitful. He was in a movie auditorium surrounded by dead men. On one side of the aisle sat rows of Viet Cong and North Vietnamese Regulars. They were covered with mud and dried blood. Some had gaping wounds with maggots squirming at the edges. On the other side were Americans. He saw John Clay, Brad Holcomb, Rat Man, Mike Delaney, the two dead specialists from Monkey Mountain, crew members whose names he could not remember, and a score of SOG reconnaissance team members, some with their Montagnard trackers sitting next to them. At the rear of the theater, pallets of aluminum coffins lined the wall. On the stage a screen flashed images of wartime carnage; the crowd cheered and whistled enthusiastically. The smell of death was overpowering. An ashen corpse sitting next to him turned, and, through purple lips, said, "Smells like somebody shit on a pile of dead monkeys in here."

A slide of Ivan Karnow, smiling, appeared and the crowd booed. A picture of Louis Good lying crumpled beneath a forklift brought a cheer. Shelly Robinson's battered body brought a scream of delight. Swollen eyes and split, bleeding lips indicated the beating she had endured. Her Red Cross uniform was torn open and covered in blood, her panties twisted around one ankle. The crowd cheered wildly.

The next slide silenced the auditorium. The only sound was the distant whoosh of the main rotor. The photo captured the pilot in mid-stride, fists clenched, mouth gasping for air, mud flying. The fear in his eyes overwhelmed the audience. The next slide was an enlargement of the first one. The tendons in his neck were stretched against his skin. A mist of sweat and rain flew from his tousled, black hair. The eyes—oh the eyes!—with their fear and sudden realization, caused Eden to look away. He scanned down his flight suit, past the captain's bars on his shoulders to the dark stitching of the long, sewn-in name tag—a long tag to accommodate the name Hallingbye.

The next slide was a blow-up of Hallingbye's right eye, grainy and distorted around the edges. But the reflection in the center of the pupil was clear. It took the crowd a moment to see it, then to comprehend it. They gasped collectively at the image of Eden in the gun bay, an orange flash emanating from the barrel of his M-60.

CHAPTER 14

"He who pretends to look on death without fear lies. All men are afraid of dying, this the great law of sentient beings, without which the entire human species would soon be destroyed."
Jean-Jacques Rousseau
La Nouvelle Heloise

5:55 a.m.

SHE LAY SLEEPING ON HER SIDE, FACING OUTWARD, ONLY the thin sheet covering her nakedness. She had stopped wearing a nightgown when Jessica left home. Eden marveled at how beautiful she still was. Only five months separated them, but she looked much younger. He had turned 57 in May. In the mornings he felt like it. He was still slim and muscular with almost as much hair as in his youth, but it was mostly gray now. Elizabeth was as trim as the day he'd first seen her. Her hair was graying, too, and she let it. The silvery streaks only accentuated her flawless skin and youthful radiance. When she smiled, her entire body smiled. He never tired of looking at her.

The dawn's quiet magnified the creaking floorboards in the hallway as he shifted his weight in the partially open doorway. Elizabeth stirred but did not awaken. He looked at her as a father looks at his daughter, with awe and respect for her individuality and with hopeful anticipation for her future. The memories of her growth in their relationship were warm and he cherished them. His eyes began to burn. When she was awake, he could never express how he felt about her. She sometimes complained that he was impenetrable, always distant. The guilt was with him constantly and he feared discovery with every waking moment. He loved her and hated himself.

There were close calls, when the moment was right for him to reveal his secrets. They would bubble up from deep within him, his heart would race and his hands tremble. At the last second he would clamp his mouth shut and swallow the black cancer that consumed him from within. Sometimes it made him physically ill to ingest the foul tasting bolus that was his past. But he could not stand the thought of betraying her image of him. It was better that he not see her at all when she learned the truth. And she would know the truth soon.

It was time, but he could not close the door. He loved watching her sleep. Sometimes after the nightmare, he would sit in the wingback reading chair and watch her. Often she would awaken and ask if he was all right. He would say that he was fine and tell her to go back to sleep. When he returned to bed, he would gently slide in next to her, touching the warmth of her body, making the slightest contact. Her body was a poultice for his anguish. As long as he touched her, he would sleep. He slowly closed the door. He was weak with grief.

In the living room he picked up the revolver and placed it in his pocket, under his shirt. He did not stop to inspect mementos. There was no more time for trips down memory lane. He had to remain focused, the way the Army had trained him. He glassed the Feds at the end of the driveway. They both watched the house. Anger, again, stirred within him. He remembered the threats and the question of his loyalty. It had been more than thirty years, and he had kept their secrets. But they still did not trust him. He doubted if the two guys in the Mazda knew what a Bright Light was. They undoubtedly were indoctrinated with the belief that national security was at risk. What was really at risk were the tarnished image of a dead president and more than a quarter-century of trust between a man and a woman.

We'll watch you, we'll test you. You fuck up, we'll kill you; he remembered the SOG colonel putting him on notice. He had spoken to no one. They viewed him as a liability and probably kept an open file, but he doubted that they had spent much time monitoring his activities. Then LaFollette had surfaced. *That poor bastard is dead meat unless Congress has him in some sort of witness protection program*, he thought. Why was he still alive, anyway? Someone who abused his body with booze and drugs the way LaFollette did should have died a long time ago.

He had spent only a few months of his life with John LaFollette, but they had been the toughest months of his tour. They had flown one Bright Light mission after another, all flyboys, all unsuccessful. By then Eden had known what their true mission was: reconnaissance, not rescue. They were forward observers, spotters for the air strikes that absolved Nixon's sins. At the time, LaFollette had had no clue of what their real mission was. He was a trigger happy wild man who delighted in strafing refugees as they squatted to relieve themselves on China Beach.

Lonnie Webster had known their mission and had been as gung ho as they got—a super-lifer. He'd shared nothing with his crew and followed orders to the letter. He would counter anything LaFollette offered to Congress and would do it credibly. The Pentagon brass would line up to refute the accusations and support Tucker. The Republican leadership would rally and claim political sabotage. A hurricane would strike, a Pakistani ferry would sink, the stock market would crash, or some other catastrophe would occur that would divert the media's attention. In the end, Senator Roberts would lose the public's interest. The hearings would fade away and so would the Senator's bid for the presidency. But the damage to Eden would be irreparable. The only things in life that he cared about were Beth and Jessica and he could not hope to recover from the loss of trust that would surely occur. More than thirty years is a long time to carry that much guilt. He was tired; relieved, in a way, that it was finally over.

Rodney crowed again, but with less enthusiasm. The sun had reached the door of the barn. It was time. His arms hung heavily from his sides and his knees felt as if they would buckle under him. Breathing was a conscious effort. *Point and pull, copper-jacketed death,* as simple as that, he thought. Point and pull. He stared at the telephone on the kitchen wall and focused on the numbers nine and one. *Three strokes to report a murder. Eden Cain killed by Richard Nixon. Send the coroner, send the sheriff, send somebody—and hurry, before my wife wakes up.*

CHAPTER 15

"All say, 'How hard it is that we have to die'—
a strange complaint to come from the mouths of people
who have had to live."
Mark Twain
Pudd'nhead Wilson

1977

WORN TENNIS SHOES PROTRUDED FROM BENEATH the frayed hem of the satin tunic. Eden thought it contradictory that God's representative, in his lustrous, purple vestments symbolizing purity and a spotless life, wore the shoes of a common man.

"Jesus Christ, who by His victory on the cross, offers the only true consolation to Carl's family in their loss and challenges them to live more faithful lives," the priest said.

Eden doubted if a more faithful life would have eased Elizabeth's grief.

The liturgy was short: no Latin, incense, or ringing of bells. Christ's body and blood were symbolically consumed.

"The Mass is both the source and the summit of our faith. Today, we celebrate Carl's death with the fullest expression of our faith in God's mercy, our hope in the resurrection of the dead, and the love that God has for us which is not interrupted, even by death." The priest smiled piously.

Eden was surprised there was minimal kneeling and recitation. Hymns were sung, throats were cleared, and children whined. Elizabeth and Jessica sat in the front pew with her Aunt Gretchen and a collection of shirttail relatives. Without a hat, her blonde hair glowed against her black sleeveless dress. Jessica, a miniature replica of her mother, sat quietly next to Elizabeth. Her head movements were animated as she oriented toward the slightest sights and sounds of the ceremony.

At Carl's request, no eulogies were offered. "It'd be just a pack of lies," he had said. "They'll be sitting there thinking how they'd love to have my bottomland and how long they should wait before making Elizabeth an offer."

The priest walked slowly down the center aisle toward the back of the church while the congregation sang the last hymn. Elmer Snyder of Snyder's Funeral Home—the one with the white clock in the center of the front arcade, its face surrounded by a green neon ring—appeared from the wings. With his back to the crowd, he deftly removed the pall, opened Carl's casket, and straightened the pillow. Starting with Elizabeth, two ushers released each pew, one at a time from either side of the aisle, to file past Carl with last respects.

Women dabbed ceremoniously at their eyes and men gave only furtive glances to Carl's emaciated and discolored corpse. He looked old, old and dead. His gray pin-striped suit with wide lapels engulfed his once robust body. Carl had only been sixty-two, but looked twenty years older. His round, Scandinavian face had withered, giving him the appearance of a mummy. He had died slowly, painfully. The melanoma had metastasized, taking his liver, then his lungs. At his request, Elizabeth had brought him home to die. Round-the-clock nursing care and morphine had kept him alive for nearly two weeks. His last words to Eden were whispered instructions on feed rations for lactating sows.

Elizabeth stood at the back of the church, a long line of people moving slowly toward her. Each took her hand; many hugged her as they offered emotional condolences. As Eden inched his way toward her, his mind raced desperately for something meaningful to say. They were lovers and the congregation knew it. Most thought it was an arranged courtship, contrived by Carl to save his farm rather than his daughter. Carl had stopped at the feed store on his way back from Burlington the day he'd received the fatal diagnosis. He'd begged Eden to work for him, to move in as hired man, to run the farm and, maybe, get to know his daughter better. Carl had not suspected that Eden and Elizabeth were seeing each other secretly, driving as far as Centerville to be out of the public's eye. When Carl had told her of his offer to Eden, she had been coy, greeting the potential arrangement with forced suspicion. A month later, Carl had finally worked up the courage to tell her of the cancer.

Eden stopped briefly in front of the casket. He could feel the cold stares of the parishioners and the silent accusations of covetous behavior, of farm and daughter. He was an outsider and always would be. He was sure the organ music was drowning out the whispers. He knew every one of them; he had served them at the feed store, talked with them at community functions. But now he was applying for membership.

Elizabeth saw him advancing toward her and quickly averted her gaze. She smiled tightly at people and nodded her acceptance of their sympathies. Aunt Gretchen received them next, each mourner soliciting new tears. Eden inched forward. He decided not to say anything. After all, he had already said it. They had talked of Carl's death for weeks before it occurred. Two years earlier, Carl acting as matchmaker, offered him a job and Eden had accepted before either he or Elizabeth knew of Carl's cancer. Carl had insisted that Eden move in, that room and board were included as employee benefits. The guest room on the first floor was comfortable and Elizabeth's cooking was a welcome improvement to the quality of his life.

She would come to him in the middle of the night, quietly slipping under the covers. With nightgown on, she would straddle him, making love to him slowly, silently, her hair tickling his face. At dawn she would tiptoe back to her room. Eden believed that Carl had known. It was difficult for Eden to act disinterested in Elizabeth, especially at breakfast when he could still smell her musky passion as she served his bacon and eggs.

Even in grief, she's the most beautiful woman on earth, he thought, as he moved slowly toward her. She would occasionally meet his stare and quickly look away. When he finally reached her, he awkwardly extended his hand. She looked down at his hand then back at him. Her eyes were swollen and red. She forced a smile, ignored his hand, and gently embraced him. "Take a breath, Eden," she whispered in his ear, then pushed herself away to receive the next mourner.

She broke down at the Committal. Eden wanted to push his way toward the grave and take her in his arms. Aunt Gretchen consoled her, pulling wadded-up tissues from her purse. He had to turn away for fear of crying himself. He could not bear to see her hurt. He stared upward at the tops of the huge, knurled oak trees, their leaves turning restlessly in the late morning breeze. He inhaled deeply through his nose. The smell of freshly mowed grass provided the distraction he needed.

"Through the committal of the body, we express our hope that Carl will experience the glory of the resurrection," the priest said. "This land is holy, set apart, blessed and consecrated for the specific purpose of burying the body."

Eden cocked his head slightly as he listened to the vibrations of the wind through limbs and leaves. It became rhythmic, whooshing and chopping through the treetops. When he became suspicious it was already too late; the apparition had begun. *From the far side of the cemetery the runner dodged between tombstones, slipping on the wet grass. Bits of turf and mud rose slowly in the air behind him as the scene played in dreamlike slow motion. Among the trees at the edge of the cemetery, dark figures moved stealthily behind the runner, from tree to tree. The fear and determination on his face was so intense that Eden was transfixed. The runner's dark, wet hair rose and fell with each slow motion step. With fists clenched and arms pumping to the sky, he ran for his life. But this time he did not run toward Eden as he always had in the past. This time he ran toward Elizabeth.*

Eden's fists slowly closed and his body became rigid with the realization that the runner intended to expose him, to tell her about Eden Cain.

The olive drab flight suit stretched at the seams as the runner turned and headed directly for her.

"We believe in the resurrection of the body and in the consummation of the world," the priest said.

The runner leaped over a horizontal headstone. The tendons in his neck bulged in straight lines, disappearing beneath the wet collar of his flight suit.

"There is life after death, and the dead are still part of the Christian community."

Elizabeth's head was bowed. She did not see the runner approaching from her right. *He reached out to her with one hand, leaning acutely forward, stumbling and begging for her recognition.*

"Though separated from this life, the dead are still at one with the community of believers on earth and benefit from their prayers."

"No!" Eden screamed, taking a step forward, his eyes wide with fear.

The priest stopped and everyone turned toward Eden. Elizabeth looked at him with a puzzled expression. The runner had vanished. People leaned toward each other and whispered. The priest cleared his throat loudly to regain the mourners' attention.

"When we are baptized, our bodies are marked with the seal of the Holy Trinity and we become the temples of the Holy Spirit. We respect and honor the bodies of the dead and their place of rest."

Eden looked down in embarrassment. People still stared at him, including Jessica. Mr. Schaeffer put his hand on Eden's shoulder to comfort him. Startled, Eden jumped and spun around, which furthered his embarrassment.

Lunch was served in the basement of the Catholic church. Everyone had brought a covered dish, but it could have been for any community event, since the food never varied. Lime Jell-O with shaved carrots, potato salad, deviled eggs sprinkled with paprika, scalloped potatoes, green bean casseroles, ham, fried chicken, and roast beef. People laughed and children who had been forced to be still now ran and played. Elizabeth was again greeted by friends and relatives, but the conversations were light and usually included a statement about how lovely the ceremony was and something about the weather. Jessica and several other children hovered over the dessert table, where Iowa cuisine was most amply represented.

Eden stood by himself at the far end of the room, sipping coffee from a Styrofoam cup. He caught Elizabeth looking at him several times, apparently worried about his outburst at the cemetery. The priest, who had shed his vestments, avoided Eden as if he were the Antichrist and instead gorged himself on homemade pickles. An Amish family whom Carl had befriended sat by themselves in the far corner of the basement. Eden thought of sitting with them, but knew that would only alienate him further from the community. Instead, he slowly worked his way toward the door and took the stairs two at a time toward the sunshine, leaving quietly. He felt guilty about leaving Elizabeth to fend for herself at the church. But it was better that way. Tongues were already wagging about their relationship and he wanted to save her further public scrutiny. They had taken separate vehicles to the funeral, but that offered little to the rumormongers who knew Eden lived in the house with Elizabeth. With their chaperone dead, they would now be viewed as living together. The Princess and the Farmhand made for good conversation in the community. Even the men at the feed store had stopped telling Eden "farmer's daughter" jokes. For two people who said they did not care what others thought, they invested much time and energy in order to appear unaffiliated.

He busied himself with chores, cussing under his breath for the stupid stunt at the cemetery. The dreams and visions were bad enough, but now he was reacting to them as if they were real. He worried that he was losing touch with reality. He muttered to himself in anger and frustration. By the time he was finished feeding the pigs, he realized he had been so self-centered that he had almost forgotten about Carl. What about Elizabeth, who had just lost her father, and Jessica, who had never experienced death before? What about them, he asked himself.

He avoided Elizabeth when she returned with Jessica late in the afternoon. He felt awkward in trying to console her, embarrassed by his behavior at the cemetery, and guilty about their living arrangement. It was best that he not impose his awkwardness upon her. She needed time to grieve, time to sort out her feelings and their relationship.

The warm shower of water beat against his eyelids and poured into his open mouth. He did not hear the bathroom door open or see Elizabeth undressing on the other side of the frosted shower door. He startled briefly when she entered the stall, a draft circling about his legs. Turning around, he wiped the water from his eyes and pushed his hair back.

"I didn't want to be alone tonight," she said, her arms folded across her breasts.

She appeared small and vulnerable, but he knew she was neither. He placed the back of his wet hand against her cheek and stared into her sad eyes.

"I'll stay with you," he said.

"I don't want to be alone tomorrow night or the next night or ever again," she said, her eyes filling with tears.

He took her into his arms and held her tightly beneath the warm spray.

"I love you, Eden," she said. But the passion in her voice was different than any time before. It was not the passion of physical love, but an emotional avowal, consummatory and final.

There was no plan, only the warm security of being totally immersed in the being of another person. He had never felt so lost, so adrift without purpose.

At 3:00 a.m., still awake, he slid quietly from bed, being careful not to disturb her. They had not made love. Instead, he had held her in his arms until she had fallen asleep. He slipped on his jeans and a T-shirt and tiptoed from the room.

Sitting on the back porch step he marveled at the brightness of the stars. The constellations appeared dimensional, having depth in the blackness of space. He had not smoked since Vietnam, but suddenly craved a cigarette. He was nervous because he knew what had to be done. Taking a deep breath, he held it until his chest burned. He stared at Orion the Hunter and then the constellations Canis Major and Taurus, as if the answer were written in the heavens.

The screen door spring stretched with a familiar whine when Elizabeth came barefoot onto the porch. She sat down next to him and pulled her ISU jersey over her knees. She, too, stared at the stars. Neither of them spoke.

"You're going to leave, aren't you?" she asked softly.

Eden continued to stare upward, his eyes glassy, moving slowly from the Hunter to the Bull.

She waited silently.

He did not look at her, but continued to gaze, seeing nothing. He swallowed discreetly.

Elizabeth rose gently and went into the house, closing the screen quietly behind her.

*****

Green fields of corn, illuminated by dawn's light, stretched endlessly in undulating patterns, separated by the asphalt ribbon before him. White farmsteads dotted the sea of green, rising obliquely from the landscape: geometric oddities that gave purpose to the uniformity. Eden drove west.

CHAPTER 16

"... any man's death diminishes me, because I am involved in mankind; and therefore never send to know for whom the bell tolls; it tolls for thee."
John Donne
Devotions Upon Emergent Occasions

1971

BRAVO BRAVO HOTEL EIGHT."

"Copy."

"Bravo Bravo Hotel Eight. Pony Boy, reporting a visual. I repeat, we have confirmation. Over."

"Roger that, Pony Boy. Stand by."

Eden leaned forward in the gun port to survey the still smoldering wreckage of the F-105 Thunderchief. The "Thud" had plowed an impressive clearing in the Laotian jungle. The Bright Light scramble had gone off at 0600 hours. The Flyboy had gone down early the previous evening.

"Bravo Bravo Hotel Eight; do you have coordinates for the Pony Boy? Over."

"Stand by, Pony Boy."

"Bubble butt rear echelon motherfucker," Lonnie Webster said. "The cheese dick thinks we can just stand by with a few tons of Huey blaring out our position to Charlie." Lonnie was starting to show the intolerance that comes with surviving too many close calls. Having to run the radio, since Command had reduced his crew by one, also made him angry.

Eden had a bad feeling about this mission—he was so short that he got a bad feeling every time he strapped in lately. But today the feeling had been particularly strong. He had been uneasy when awakened by the headquarters runner who scrambled the crew. He'd awakened with an erection so hard that a cat couldn't scratch it. In his dream he'd been making love to the cute donut dolly he had met earlier in the week. Like the heroine in the book she had given him to read, she had been distraught over losing her husband, a pilot, and Eden had only meant to comfort her. But in her grief, she had become passionate, then naked. He'd known it was wrong, but could not stop. At the most critical moment of his uncontrolled ecstasy, her husband had appeared, taken him by the shoulder, and said, "Cain, roll out. You've been scrambled for 0600."

"Echo Echo River Six."

"You got the Pony Boy," Lonnie said.

"Recon Voodoo reports a parachute at one six degrees north, one zero seven west. Over."

"Roger that, Bravo Bravo." Lonnie pitched the chopper sharply to the west. "Shit, that narrows it down to about a thousand square miles," he mumbled into the intercom.

"Hope he's got smoke," LaFollette said.

"Hope he's got a goddamned chainsaw to hack out an LZ in that shit," co-pilot Brian Levy said.

They flew a grid pattern at a thousand meters, looking for the parachute against the green canopy below. A small river with wide serpentine arcs snaked through the jungle, providing arable land along its floodplain. Narrow paddocks of rice, light green rectangles separated by mud dikes, appeared at the jungle's edge.

"Bravo Bravo Hotel Eight," Lonnie called.

"We copy, Pony Boy. Over."

"Bravo Bravo, has there been radio contact? Over."

"Negative on the radio contact, Pony Boy."

"Roger. We're negative on the silk. Over."

"You're getting warm, Pony Boy. A Birddog is reporting signal movement in the vicinity. We're trying to get a fix. Over."

"Why the hell are we looking for a parachute if the Bird's collared?"

"Stand by, Pony Boy."

They continued their search pattern, Lonnie eyeing the fuel gauge. "Tell you what, boys," he said. "At this altitude, Flyboy would be reluctant to pop smoke, especially if he's got dinks chasing his ass. Let's fly those paddies at two hundred meters and see if we can draw some smoke."

"We'll draw more than smoke," LaFollette said.

On the first pass above the river, muzzle flashes appeared from the jungle's edge and tracer rounds surrounded them.

"Looks like Chuck is hunting our Flyboy, too," Lonnie said.

"They probably gathered up his silk. They knew we'd be right behind. Hope they don't have any recoilless set up yet," Levy said.

At the end of the paddy run, Lonnie banked sharply and came around for a second pass. He knew by Charlie's presence that Flyboy had to be close, if they had not yet caught him. He noticed the dark gray cloud bank rolling down from the highlands, black streaks of rain slanting with the wind toward the ground.

"Cowboy, give 'em what for on this pass," Lonnie said.

Eden locked his M-60 with the first round. Automatic rifle fire erupted from the tree line, white-orange flashes from the green darkness. "There must be an entire company down there," he said, holding his microphone button down.

The Huey came in low and fast as he positioned Eden for the assault. Tracers flashed by the Plexiglas cockpit. Eden opened fire, strafing the tree line, his own tracers disappearing toward the muzzle flashes. The chopper's speed was so great that he had no time for a reverse strafe. As they ended the pass and banked east for the return, a plume of red smoke rose upward from a grassy area between the jungle and rice paddies to the east, less than three hundred meters from Charlie.

"Smoke at nine o'clock!" Eden yelled.

"Bravo Bravo Hotel Eight, forget the coordinates; we have smoke, but need air support. Over," Lonnie radioed.

"Negative on the air support, Pony Boy. The nearest covey has an ETA of forty-seven minutes. Over."

"Bravo Bravo, he doesn't have forty-seven minutes. The dinks are on him like chickens on a June bug. They're looking to grease his ass. Over."

"Stand by."

"*Stand by*," Lonnie said with total disbelief over the intercom. "You new meat piece of dog shit. Who the hell is running this war?" Lonnie positioned for another pass. "Roach Face, it's your turn. Cowboy, see if you can spot the runner."

Charlie had their number this time. The first pass had been for practice. They knew how far to lead with their AK-47s. Rounds ricocheted through the cockpit and slammed into the armor plated floor. LaFollette whooped and screamed with the same intensity as when he played pinball at the Enlisted Men's Club.

"Echo Echo River Six. Do you read? Over."

"Stand by. We're in the middle of a war here," Lonnie said.

At the end of the second pass, they swung wide over the jungle to avoid Charlie's potshots.

"What'd you see, Cowboy?" Lonnie asked.

"Didn't eyeball the runner, but the gooks are swarming toward his smoke," Eden said.

"Echo Echo River Six."

"This is Pony Boy. We copy, Bravo Bravo. Over."

"Pony Boy, this is the C.O. of JPRC. Go to secured frequency. Over."

"Roger."

Eden's headset went dead as Lonnie turned off the intercom and switched to the secured frequency. Its transmissions were supposed to be secure from monitoring. Something big was going down for the Commanding Officer of the Joint Personnel Recovery Center to get on the horn.

"Bravo Bravo Hotel Eight, Come in, Bravo Bravo. Over."

"We copy, Pony Boy. Command and Control North has just ordered a sterile Bright Light. Do you read? Over."

Lonnie did not respond immediately. The JPRC apparently knew from reconnaissance that Charlie was strong in the area. He looked down at the plume of red smoke, now dissipating, and the black figures of men moving toward it. He looked at Brian Levy and shook his head. "That poor bastard down there is hunkered down in some bushes, scared and armed with nothing but a 45 Auto." His jaw tightened with anger. "Bravo Bravo, we copy, but are unable to comply without air support. Over."

"Pony Boy, you will comply. That is a direct order, Mister. You will remove the target without unnecessary risk. Mop-up is on the way. Do you read? Over."

"Without unnecessary risk" meant that they were not to attempt a rescue. The last thing SOG wanted was a downed chopper and captured crew in Laos. That would make a bad situation downright embarrassing. The JPRC knew they had nothing but smoke grenades and a couple of M-60s. They did not have the fire power to sterilize anything, except the pilot. An air strike was on the way, not as an offensive measure; rather, as an insurance policy that Charlie did not end up with a walking, talking

American pilot. The brass at CCN would take no chances. They had used Lonnie as a spotter before, dropping red smoke for the F-4s, F-100s, and Skyraiders to hone in on, delivering their total devastation. But somebody had screwed up this time and the covey had not been dispatched in time. Charlie had arrived first and they wanted to feed their propaganda machine with a live pilot. The Old Man at DaNang wanted a confirmed kill and was not willing to bet Nixon his Three Stars that Charlie would not end up with a new TV personality. If the mop-up went sour, the worst that could happen would be Chuck ending up with a dead pilot. Dead guys were not much of a threat to the politicians. "Bravo Bravo Hotel Eight. You're breaking up. Say again. Over. Might as well make the bastards sweat a little," Lonnie added under his breath.

"Echo Echo River Six. Do you copy? Over."

Lonnie turned on the intercom. "Cowboy, got a visual?"

"Negative," Eden said.

"Roach Face?"

"Just smoke," LaFollette said.

"Tell you what, boys, we'll make a slow, low pass over the smoke to draw our boy out. Charlie may only give us one shot, so be alert. I'll come in on your side, Cowboy. Roach Face, the resistance will be on our flank. Lay the shit down heavy."

"Echo Echo River Six. Come in, Pony Boy." The C.O. was sounding a little frantic.

"Just once I'd like to get one of those ring-knocking, super-lifers on a real combat mission to show them war, to let them hear and smell war; to put faces on people instead of moving pins with little flags on them around a big map in the security of a deep bunker at Marble Mountain," Lonnie said, looking straight ahead.

"Echo Echo River Six."

Lonnie turned the volume of the radio down. He needed to concentrate in order to get Flyboy out alive.

As soon as they reached the jungle's edge, Lonnie dropped to treetop altitude and headed for the smoke. A rocket with a smoky tail slid beneath the chopper's belly. It lumbered toward them, compared to the rounds from the automatic weapons that sped past them. Charlie swarmed below them, animated dark figures rushing with collective force toward the smoke. Eden could see their uniforms and recognized them as North Vietnamese Army regulars. It's rare to see Viet Cong anymore, he thought. The VC that were left seemed to be stragglers who sniped from remote villages and rarely crossed into Laos.

"Lay it down, Roach Face," Lonnie said, bringing the Huey broadside to the onslaught.

LaFollette commenced firing. Eden could not see him, but knew by the nonstop, full auto chatter of his M-60 that he had plenty to shoot at.

The red smoke quickly dissipated as the chopper hovered over the site, twisting restlessly at the stinging rounds of AK-47 fire.

It had started to rain.

"Come out, come out, wherever you are," Eden nervously recited to himself as he scanned the grassy interface with the jungle.

"Echo Echo River Six. Come in, Pony Boy. Over."

Rounds ricocheted dangerously within the bay of the helicopter. Eden saw movement at the tree line on his flank, followed by muzzle flashes. He opened fire in an attempt to slow Charlie's advancement, but now realized the dinks were both upstream and downstream of the smoke. Another rocket sliced through the sky, narrowly missing the Huey's tail section. Bullets slapped against the hull. "We're taking it hard on the starboard side," Eden said into the intercom, between bursts of machine gun fire.

Lonnie spun the chopper 180 degrees and flew a tight circle so that Eden ended up with the same perspective, but briefly became a moving target.

"Echo Echo River Six. Over."

"Any sign of Flyboy?" Lonnie shouted.

Both LaFollette and Eden were too busy to respond.

"We can't take any more of this shit. Our ass is hanging in the breeze, boys," Lonnie said.

Eden saw him first as he emerged running from the dark edge of the jungle. He was hunkered down in an attempt to present a lower profile. "Flyboy at two o'clock!" Eden yelled.

Lonnie edged the helicopter toward the advancing runner and dropped altitude. Bullets shattered the windshield. He twisted to port, putting Eden at 90 degrees to Flyboy. LaFollette continued to lay down fire on full auto.

"Jesus Christ," Lonnie said. "Run, goddamn it."

Clods of mud flew head-high behind the pilot as he slipped, going down on one hand, then righting himself. Frantically, Eden fired over the pilot's head at the advancing NVA. For every one he dropped, two more appeared from the jungle. It was now raining much harder, steam rising from Eden's barrel.

"Echo Echo River Six."

Flyboy's olive drab flight suit was muddy and torn. His dark, wet hair rose and fell with each step. Tracers flew above his head, aimed at the chopper, not him. Charlie wanted this boy alive, Eden realized, rounds slamming into his gun port. The runner was close enough that Eden could see the fear and determination on his face. Eden quickly glanced at Lonnie to see if he, too, was tracking the runner. Lonnie, instead, was pushing Levy's body off the stick. The cockpit was splattered with blood.

"Set it down!" Eden screamed above the noise of his own machine gun.

Another rocket passed less than a foot in front of them.

"I'm hit, I'm hit!" LaFollette yelled into the intercom, his M-60 suddenly silent.

"Echo Echo River Six. Come in, Pony Boy. Over."

Eden could see the expression change on Flyboy's face as the pilot sensed his liberation. He was thirty meters out and his expression was now pure determination, the fear replaced with hope. Eden sprayed a line of running NVA less than eighty meters out.

Black smoke began pouring from the exhaust shroud of the turbo jet. Eden could smell the burning oil.

"Hump your ass, Flyboy!" Lonnie yelled.

"Set it down," Eden said, still firing.

"Echo Echo, do you copy?"

"Oh God, I'm hit bad. I'm hit real bad!" LaFollette cried.

Lonnie twisted in his seat to look around the radio console to check on LaFollette. The gun port appeared empty. LaFollette lay crumpled in the corner, stretched against his tether. Blood was flowing between the fingers of his right hand, which he kept clutched to his side. "Roach Face, you cheese dick, light yourself a joint. It'll make you feel better. You're going to be fine. Looks like a goddamned flesh wound."

"Set it down, Lonnie!" Eden yelled.

As Lonnie brought the nose up, the rotor's downwash filled the cabin with dark smoke. "Cowboy, it's me and you and a helluva lot of gooks."

Eden did not respond. He was too busy killing people. AK rounds punched through the aluminum bulkhead, inches from his face. The rain came down in sheets, making the advancing NVA appear fuzzy around the edges, unfocused dark spots.

"Rocket at five o'clock!" Lonnie screamed.

Turning to his right, Eden saw Charlie standing boldly with the launcher on his shoulder, his head tilted as he aimed through the elevated sights. Eden swung instinctively toward him, the first burst catching him squarely in the midsection. As the soldier fell he triggered the rocket into the ground beside him. An orange ball of fire with a shower of pink sparks burst over Flyboy's head.

"Echo Echo River Six. Come in. Over."

Lonnie tapped a gauge on the panel in front of him. He looked to his right. Flyboy had fallen and was struggling to his feet in the mud and rain. A continuous line of NVA had formed in front of him and to the right. Muzzle flashes exploded up and down the line of advancing enemy. He could feel the sting of bullets riddling the chopper's hull.

"Oh fuck, I'm bleedin' real bad," LaFollette said weakly.

"Pony Boy, do you copy? Over."

The sickening smell of burning oil filled the cockpit.

"Set it down, Lonnie," Eden said, his M-60 exploding continuously.

The Huey pitched and yawed uncontrollably as Lonnie clutched at his right knee. The bullet had entered on the lower right side of his thigh and exited above and to the left of his knee cap. Blood flowed warmly down his leg. Lonnie panted with pain, crying out when he attempted to stabilize the chopper with the subtle movements of the foot treadles. Levy's body suddenly pitched forward from the impact of a round that hit him squarely in the back of his head. Milky white brain tissue covered the inside of his visor, his head bobbing lifelessly.

Flyboy fell again, this time so close that the rotor's downwash seemed to disorient him as he struggled to his feet. Wind-driven rain pelted him with such intensity that he could not open his eyes. He cupped both hands over his eyes in an attempt to locate the chopper.

"Set it down, Lonnie!" Eden yelled again.

"Cowboy," Lonnie said into the intercom, followed by a long pause. "I'm hit and we're losing oil pressure fast. We've gotta *di di mau* or we're going down in this hornet's nest." He paused again; the Huey pitched restlessly. "Eden, I want you to grease the Flyboy. That's an order straight from the top."

Eden continued to fire. "Lonnie, set this goddamned Bird down. He's here. Ten feet lower and he can grab a skid, for Christ's sake."

"That's an order, Cowboy. Do you hear me? Shoot the bastard." Lonnie began to climb while slowly drifting away from the advancing pilot.

The runner reached out toward the retreating helicopter, a gesture begging for help. Eden saw the change of expression that swept over his face, from fearful determination to total desperation, a man slowly slipping over the edge of a cliff. He was so close that Eden could see his rank and name tag. His captain's bars were sewn to his shoulders and the name Hallingbye stretched over the left side of his chest. The look on his face caused Eden to stop firing. It was a look that stopped the action, the sights and sounds of war. There was nothing else, only Captain Hallingbye and Eden, their eyes locked in total silence. Water flew in a mist from the Captain's tousled black hair, his arms pumped with clenched fists. It was his eyes that silenced the world, his eyes that held Eden motionless; eyes that Eden had known for a thousand years. He reached out again to Eden, desperate and searching. His mouth opened and the word "No" formed on his lips as his only hope rose slowly away from him and he felt himself slip over the edge.

"Fire," Lonnie ordered. Bullets riddled the chopper from every direction, black smoke poured from the engine.

"Echo Echo River Six."

"Fire, goddamn it! Fire, fire!" Lonnie screamed.

His voice seemed distant to Eden, garbled and thick. *Point and pull,* he said to himself. *It's the bullet that does the killing.* Point and pull.

"Fire, fire, fire!"

The runner's expression changed quickly from hopeless desperation to shock, then betrayal, as Eden swung the M-60 on him. He only wanted to know why.

The world was silent. The machine gun made no sound as it shuddered in Eden's hands.

CHAPTER 17

"Sometime in February, when the snow and sleet have shut out from the wearied mind even the memory of spring, the man of the woods generally receives his first inspiration."
Stewart Edward White
The Forest

1972

IN WYOMING, WINTER GIVES WAY TO SPRING BEGRUDGingly. May in the high country can be especially unpredictable. When Eden had unloaded the horses two days earlier, it had been sixty degrees; sunny, with the promise of summer reflected by the green on the lower meadows. But it had started snowing during the night. Nearly twenty inches had fallen and it was still coming down hard. The thermometer outside the cabin window read twenty-six degrees and the wind was beginning to push the snow into heavy drifts. He would be there longer than he had planned.

Being snowbound pleased him. It made him comfortable in the same way that pulling the covers up to his chin on a cold winter night did. He felt secure. There were plenty of dry goods on the shelves and enough firewood stacked in the loafing shed to last a month. He did worry about feed for the horses, having less than a bale of hay and half a sack of grain. If he had to, he could turn them out and they would work their way down the mountain to the lower meadows.

Eden had processed out of the Army at Fort Lewis in mid-March. Hue had fallen, Quang Tri was under siege, and the NVA were headed for Da Nang. Nixon had proudly proclaimed that Vietnamization was a success as America withdrew and the ARVN were slaughtered.

He'd sat in the Seattle-Tacoma Airport for a day and a half, not knowing where to go. He had eventually used the ticket to Denver that the Army had given him. At Stapleton he had called his father and asked him to pick him up at the bus station in Laramie. The three hour drive to the ranch had used up all the conversation that was needed. He had been gone for nearly two years and there was little to talk about. His parents were uncomfortable around him. At the ranch, his father seldom spoke and his mother pushed food at him constantly. It had taken him a while to realize that he had changed, and his parents were reacting to him in the same way they would to a stranger. They had seemed relieved when he announced that he was going to the cabin for a few days.

He needed time to think, to organize his life, and to forget. He needed time to heal. Planning was easy. Forgetting was impossible. He had boxed up everything associated with the Army, but people would not let him forget. Folks around Saratoga and Encampment gave him a wide berth. No dogs, no minors, no veterans seemed to be the attitude. He overheard conversations spilling from the bar at the Wolf about the dope-crazed, baby-killing losers that had handed America her first military loss. The news media morbidly tracked the country's embarrassment, while Nixon positioned himself for declaring a just peace.

Not knowing what to do with his life, he applied to graduate school at the University of Wyoming. He was eagerly accepted by a professor who had befriended him as an undergraduate. The switch from Animal Science to Plant Science would be challenging, and that was what he needed to help him forget. But down deep, he knew he would never forget. The dreams would always be there at night, the visions during the day.

The Army wanted him to forget. Two days of debriefing at Command and Control North, buried within XXIV Corps at Marble Mountain, had refreshed his memory of everything he was told to forget. A weasel-faced major had tried to intimidate him with threats of imprisonment if he ever compromised national security by talking about SOG. It seemed there was no distinction between national security and Nixon's public image. They were angry that he was getting out. SOG had the highest mortality rate of any unit in the history of U.S. warfare. That was the only honorable way to leave. Eden signed paper after paper agreeing not to do the things that threatened them. Consorting with Communists was high on their list of don'ts. To his knowledge, he had never talked to a Commie, and the ones he had been introduced to he had killed.

Split wood was stacked high on the covered front porch. Leaning over the porch rail, Eden strained to see the horses between the snow-laden squalls. In the fading light, he could make out their dark figures peering out from the loafing shed, their ears forward.

Snow stuck to his hair and eyelashes. He captured a few flakes on his tongue, breathing in the cold wet air. The snow left a metallic taste on the roof of his mouth. He closed his eyes and felt the cold tickles of flakes on his cheeks. He remembered the shouts and laughter of children so vividly that he thought could hear them in the distance. He felt the excitement of the playground snowball fight. It was 1957 and he wore the new wool coat his mother had ordered for his tenth birthday. He could smell the wet wool as he wiped his nose on the sleeve; steam rose from his mouth. Jimmy Talbot lay writhing in the snow, his hands clutched to his face as the crowd gathered above him. The rock Eden had packed into his snowball had cut Jimmy deep above his left eye; blood flowed down his face and neck. Jimmy screamed like a girl when the playground monitor attempted to inspect the wound.

That evening, in the cold darkness, Eden had stood beside his father on the Talbot's front porch, waiting for someone to answer his knock. When the school had called John Cain to ask that he pick up his suspended son, he'd done so without protest. After dinner he'd asked Eden to get his coat and hat. On their way to the Talbot ranch, he had turned to Eden and said, "You know what's right and you know what needs to be done." Eden knew. His apology to Mr. and Mrs. Talbot was sincere and easier than the one offered to Jimmy, who wanted to know why that old guy, Walter Lance, always appeared at the beginning of a Woody Woodpecker cartoon. John Cain had paid Mr. Talbot for the seven stitches and said that he would drop Eden by in the morning to help feed. No more was ever said of the incident.

In the yellow glow of the cabin's kerosene lamp, the fire crackling loudly, Eden knew what was right and what had to be done.

CHAPTER 18

"If the world ever learns that it knows nothing
yet about what keeps men and women loving each other,
then will it have a chance for some brief happiness
before the eternal frozen night sets in?"
Sinclair Lewis
Cass Timberlane

1977

LIFE IS NOT A SINGLE EPOCH, BUT A CONTINUUM OF MILEstones that mark one's progress toward death, Eden thought as he stared above the steering wheel of the parked Willys. He had stopped short of Nebraska and parked next to a cemetery on the hilly outskirts of Shenandoah. *Each chapter ends with a goodbye, a ceremony, sometimes a reflection. How many times have I promised to keep in touch?* he asked himself. People and things moved quickly through his life with a wispy grace that barely stirred the air. Since Vietnam, he realized in advance how transitory his associations were likely to be. He kept people and things at arm's length, relationships in perspective. He braced for the trauma of saying goodbye. Graduations, wars, deaths, and relocations, each punctuated by a goodbye, were some of the markers along that continuum. He remembered the beginnings and endings clearly; the middles were often cloudy. But beginnings and endings provided contrasts when concluding another chapter. It was the last chapter of which he was certain. The next had neither title nor outline. He rolled down the window and let the warm, late summer breeze tousle his hair. The freshness hinted of new beginnings, the next installment. Eden ran his fingers through his hair and took a deep breath. He knew the previous chapter was unfinished. He did not know how it would end, but he needed to be with her when it did. Gravel spun from beneath the Jeep's tires and they gave a short yelp when they met the asphalt highway. Looking at his watch, he calculated he would be back in Keotonka just before dark.

*****

"How far did you get?" Elizabeth asked, her eyes red and puffy from crying.

"Far enough to realize that I had made a mistake," Eden said.

"How big of a mistake?" she asked, wiping a tear from her eye then folding her arms across her chest.

"It was a mistake of gigantic proportion," he said, smiling slightly.

"You should have kept going," she said, turning away from him and clutching the sides of the kitchen sink. "It seems that everyone I've ever cared about has left: my husband, my mother, my father, now my lover. If you value your life, you better get away from me."

"I do value my life, that's why I came back. I love you, Beth. I can't imagine my life without you. I didn't leave for me, I left for you. I'm not the man you think I am. You don't know me. It's time you find out who the real Eden Cain is. I want to tell you things. I want to share with you the horrible things I have done."

She turned to face him, tears flowing down her cheeks. "Eden, don't—"

"I have to tell you. I rehearsed my confession all the way back here. You need to know who I am and what I've done. And when you find out, you'll want me out of your life forever. But at least there will be no what-ifs, no questions left unanswered. You'll know you did the right thing and you can get on with your life. And I can get on with mine. But, I can't live with the guilt and the nightmares anymore. I have to tell you. It's time to let you know, time to say goodbye."

"Is it about Vietnam?"

"Yes."

"Then I don't want to hear it," she said.

"Nobody wants to hear about it. The whole damn country doesn't want to hear about it. Everybody acts like it never happened. But it did happen, Beth. It still happens. Every day it happens to me. It's who I am now."

"It's not relevant to us. It won't change my feelings for you. There is nothing that you can say—"

"Yes there is, Beth. You need to hear it and I need to tell you."

She turned away from him and stared out the kitchen window. "I love you, Eden. I don't want to lose you. I don't want to hear anything that will make me lose you. Please, Eden, I'm begging you." She turned to face him. Her lower lip quivered and tears streaked her cheeks. "If you love me, then don't tell me anything that would take you away from me."

He stared into her swollen eyes, exhaled loudly through his nose, turned away, and turned back again. He was ready to tell her. He had prepared himself emotionally and now she refused to hear it. When would he get the relief he needed? He shook his head in frustration. Eden stepped across the kitchen and took her in his arms and held her head to his chest. "I'm sorry," he whispered. "This has been a rough week for you. Forgive me."

The moon was full and shone through the lace curtains of Elizabeth's bedroom. For the first time, she had taken him to her room. They made love, not for themselves, but for each other. It was not sex; rather, an affirmation of their feelings, a physical commitment to each other. He believed the experience was what clerics referred to as the union of man and woman. The bond was formed.

She lay on her side next to him. The white sheet seemed to glow in the moonlight, her tan leg protruding from beneath. He stared at the soft, golden reflection of her hair that spilled across her pillow to his. The nearly transparent delicateness of her ear was backlit by the window's light. He studied the prominence of her cheek bone, the squareness of her shoulders, and the curvature of her hips beneath the sheets. A light breeze fluttered the curtains, causing a kaleidoscope of moonbeams to dance over her body. He knew then he would never tell her, never leave her again.

*****

The late October sun was bright against a blue sky. The cottonwoods along the river had turned uniformly yellow. A few hickory and white oaks offered reds and browns to the season. Jessica cranked her Snoopy fishing reel, pulling her line and bobber onto shore.

"Can't catch fish unless your hook's in the water," Eden said.

"I think she's bored," Elizabeth said.

"Me too," he said. "Bored with this easy life; nothing to do all day but lie in the sun eating ham sandwiches and fishing."

Elizabeth looked out over the river. She smiled and squinted against the harsh reflection of the sun off the water. Neither of them had taken a day off since Carl had died the previous summer. They had finished picking the corn the day before. The harvest had been better than expected, with an average yield of over two hundred bushels per acre. The soybean harvest had been equally good. Prices were up and the industry was optimistic. The Washington bureaucrats preached market expansion and urged farmers to plant fence row to fence row. The optimism fueled spending; spending fueled optimism. The equipment dealer's sudden prosperity was further proof that agriculture had turned the corner to economic recovery. With Carl's death, the bank was nervous about the yearly operating loan they had given him. They seemed reluctant to extend credit for the coming season. The farm loan officer had stared blankly at Elizabeth when she had laid out their annual plan. It appeared they would have to use some of Carl's life insurance money for the next year's operating budget. Elizabeth would have to prove her credit worthiness with production figures of her own. The loan officer had been condescending and chauvinistic.

"So, let me get this straight," Elizabeth had said to him. "To get a line of credit in my name, I need to get either a husband, grow a penis, or crawl in the sack with your fat ass? Is that what you're telling me, Roger? A dozen years ago when you were sticking your tongue down my throat, you would have robbed this bank in order to get into my pants."

Eden had had to escort her from the bank before she went over the guy's desk.

Neighbors offered help during harvest, but little was accepted. Mostly they offered speculation to each other about Eden and Elizabeth's relationship. They seldom went to town together. While picking up supplies at the feed store, Mr. Schaeffer had taken Eden aside and said, "It's none of my business, son, but—"

"You're right, Mr. Schaeffer," Eden had said, cutting him off mid-sentence, looking him squarely in the eye, and smiling.

Jessica attempted to cast her line back into the river but forgot to push the line release. The bobber and worm splashed loudly inches from shore.

"How about you, are you really bored, too?" Elizabeth said.

Without looking at her, he said, "I've been too busy to be bored. But that's not what you really want to know, is it?"

"I want to know if you're happy. I want to know what your plans are. Where are we going?" she said.

The uncertainty in their lives was troubling to him, too. But he never spoke of it. It caused tightness in his stomach and a trembling in his hands. It was obvious she wanted to talk about the future. He did not answer her.

A week earlier he had opened the telephone bill and discovered four calls to Washington, D.C. made over a two-day period and a call to Minneapolis. There had been letters, incoming calls, and muffled conversations. He found her crying in the middle of the day and she offered no explanation.

Eden cast Jessica's line into the river. An Amish buggy crossed the bridge, the horses' hooves clattering loudly on the wooden planking. Eden waved to the bonneted women and they nodded their recognition.

He sat down next to Elizabeth, his shoulder touching hers. "Are you warm enough?" he asked.

"I'm fine. It's a beautiful morning."

"Beth, you know I'm not the best communicator. But I am a good listener. When you're ready to talk, I'll be right here at your side."

She pushed against his shoulder then looked away toward Jessica, who was tossing sticks into the river and singing softly to herself. Turning back to him, her eyes clouded with tears, she said, "Thanks." A wisp of blonde hair blew across her forehead. "I don't know where to start. I don't know what to feel anymore."

Eden smiled at her reassuringly, but did not speak.

"Without hope, life can be pretty depressing," she said. "Jessica and you are all that's left. I don't know where I'd be if it weren't for you. For six years I haven't been allowed to think about the future. My life has been on hold."

Jessica was singing a nursery rhyme that caused goose-flesh to form on Eden's arms: "Pony Boy, Pony Boy, won't you be my Pony Boy?"

Elizabeth turned toward Eden. "Why haven't you ever asked me about my husband?"

Eden was surprised by the hint of accusation in her voice. "I figured you would tell me when you were ready," he said.

"No, I've tried to talk with you, but you always stop me. I've been ready for a long time. There's something else."

He looked away, staring across the river. He said nothing and neither did she. She wanted an answer. "I guess I was afraid to hear what you had to say," he said.

Still, she said nothing. She waited for more.

"Beth, I've loved you from the moment I first saw you. You were, and still are, the most important thing in my life. I couldn't bear to hear you talk about him. You're the only person I have truly loved, and I want to spend the rest of my life with you. It's taken me some time to realize that you married the love of *your* life." He looked away and said nothing for a long moment. Without turning back to her he said, "You had a life before I met you. I know that. You've loved before. The details would be painful, so I didn't ask."

"But I wanted you to ask. I needed you to ask. Yes, I've loved before, but I love you now. All of you, past and present."

She paused and looked away. "I wish I could be certain about the future."

He could see her pain, but could not fully comprehend what she had suffered for the past six years. He turned toward Jessica, who squatted on the sandy embankment. She had built a miniature round corral with small rocks, neatly aligned in a near-perfect circle. In the center of the pen she had placed Dino, the goofy-looking plastic dinosaur from the Flintstone family. She was feeding it blades of dried grass and humming softly to herself. Her tiny legs, still brown from the summer's sun, disappeared into her thick-soled sneakers. Her blonde hair hung over her shoulders and she held her knees against her chest. Eden was struck by the ingenuity of her corral and the stick foundation of the nearby barn. "There's your future," he said with assurance, nodding toward Jessica.

Elizabeth turned toward Jessica and smiled. "What about you? What's your future?" she asked, turning back to him.

He did not answer.

A light breeze stirred the yellow leaves of the cottonwoods. They rustled uniformly, decaying reminders of a past life, their bones clattering lifelessly together. It was a pleasant sound, Eden thought, the kind he liked to listen to at night through the open bedroom window. It was not a symphony, no tribute to a life well-lived, just the hissing of air across the corpses of the past. Soon they would fall to the ground to tumble without control toward their future, some into the river to be carried mercifully downstream, some ground softly and deposited to enrich the next generation.

He smiled knowingly at her and she knew his answer.

CHAPTER 19

"It was an ugly thing, quickly concealed,
like a belch turned hastily into a cough,
deceiving no one."
Edna Ferber
Come and Get It

1978

THE SATURDAY EVENING CROWD NEARLY FILLED THE Keotonka café. Babies cried, farmers deaf from age and machinery talked too loudly, girls giggled, and mothers scolded. The clatter of silverware on china and the shouts of waitresses to cooks rang in Eden's ears.

"I believe Iowans are louder than hogs at feeding time," he said.

Elizabeth smiled at him from across the table, its top still sticky from the previous customers. She more than smiled, Eden thought. She glowed. He smiled back and they both inhaled deeply, their eyes locked on each other. She wore a white, spring dress with a bowed neckline. A short choker of large pearls accented her slender neck. A dark, navy sweater was draped over her shoulders for the unpredictable March nights. He, too, was overdressed for the Keotonka crowd. His white shirt and tie announced a special occasion.

The restaurant appeared brighter than usual, awash with color. The miles of philodendrons hanging from the ceiling were interspersed with hanging baskets of cheap, artificial flowers, mostly red. Red Naugahyde booths and panels topped with red and blue plastic flowers gave the place a Mexican restaurant appearance.

"Look at this place," he said. "Have you ever noticed the garage sale decor?

"I beg your pardon. This is called Art Nouveau. Where else can you find a Mona Lisa hanging next to pictures of Humphrey Bogart and Winnie the Pooh?" she asked, looking around. "You may think those porcelain figurines atop the sneeze board of the salad bar are offensively gaudy. But think again, Eden. It's true Keotonkan. Where else can you find a huge, ugly wristwatch with a twelve-inch face serving as the restaurant clock?"

"I do like the John Deere barbecue apron hanging on the wall," he said.

A young waitress, high school age, took their order. Between catfish and pork tenderloin sandwiches, the choices were limited. Arlene, their usual waitress, was busy smacking her gum and cuffing the high school boys for cussing. Eden studied the crowd and noted the number of young girls with babies. In the next booth a young father with a sparse, silky mustache wiped his mouth on his own shoulder. He counted the number of male patrons then counted again. With his finger scribbling invisible numbers on the place mat, he calculated that 84 percent of the men had their caps on.

"This is not what I envisioned," he said.

"It's okay. Maybe when we're done planting we can take a few days and go someplace nice," she said.

They said very little during the meal. The crowd noise seemed distant as they stared at each other across the table. Eden glanced at the table he had sat at four years earlier when he'd first seen Elizabeth. He remembered the lightness he'd felt in his chest and his inability to take his eyes from her as she and Jessica had danced. If she had changed in those four years, it was for the better. He believed she was even more beautiful now. Jessica had changed dramatically, losing her babyish characteristics to those of an eight-year-old. He looked at his own hands, callused and grease-stained; a blackened nail from the grain auger was his latest injury. Aside from the suntan highlights of crow's feet around his eyes and better definition to his upper body muscles, he believed he had changed little, as well. His farmer tan never seemed to fade. He had been embarrassed by his two-tone complexion the previous summer when he and Elizabeth had gone skinny dipping, then chased each other naked through the woods in the middle of the day.

Arlene suddenly appeared at their table as they finished their meals. Chewing her gum with an open mouth, she looked long at each of them. "I just want you to know how happy I am for the both of you," she said finally, her eyes becoming glassy. "It's about time. Maybe now folks will move on to a new victim, pick the eyeballs out of somebody else."

"How did you know?" Elizabeth said with surprise.

"Judge Olson takes his dinner in here every Saturday night. Eats the same damn thing every week, hot beef sandwich."

Eden shook his head. "No secrets in Keotonka," he said.

"No nothing in Keotonka," Arlene said. "Why in the world would you bring your new bride to this shithole on your wedding night?"

Eden grinned. "We wanted to share our happiness with you, Arlene."

"Horseshit," she said.

"It was spur of the moment," Elizabeth said. "We really didn't plan ahead. We wanted it simple and private."

"Private," Arlene scoffed, smiling with only one side of her mouth. "Not even your underwear is private in this town." She looked at Eden critically. "So, Cowboy, what romantic plan do you have for your honeymoon?"

"Well, after this delightful meal, I thought we'd walk over to the Texaco station and buy some Tums. Then maybe stroll to the center of the highway bridge and have a spitting contest."

"We've reserved the suite at the Garfield," Elizabeth said, beaming.

"How romantic," Arlene said flatly. "Maybe a little dancing at the VFW would provide some memories of this momentous occasion." She stared at them again, working her gum from one side of her mouth to the other. "I'm surprised you didn't bring Jessica with you, it being your wedding night and all."

"She's at a sleepover at the Gudmunson place," Elizabeth said.

Eden believed there was a hint of defensiveness in her voice. They had not told Jessica of their plan. Elizabeth had insisted they tell her afterward. He had not questioned her decision, just told her that she should tell Jessica at the appropriate time.

"You kids want some dessert?" Arlene asked.

"No thanks, just the check, please. We're sort of anxious to get over to the Texaco station." Eden smiled.

Arlene's eyes filled with tears that spilled onto her cheeks. She hugged Elizabeth, then Eden. "There's no check. I wish you kids all the happiness in the world." Dabbing at her eyes, she spun around suddenly and disappeared into the kitchen.

The cool night air was refreshing as they stepped from the cafe. Elizabeth put her sweater on. They held hands for the first time in public as they walked down the street. Music—acoustic guitar and drums—spilled from the open door of the VFW Club. Black Magic Marker on a white board proclaimed that Randy Andy and the Stink Baits were playing tonight. Eden could smell cigarette smoke and stale beer as they approached. A man and woman stumbled from the door onto the sidewalk. The man was rough looking with long, greasy hair topped with a sweat-stained ball cap with a pheasant embroidered on the front. He wore a camouflage jacket with the sleeves ripped off and dirty blue jeans. A tattoo graced his upper arm. The wormy-looking woman appeared anorexic. Her stringy bleached hair hung in her face. Her eyes were glassy with an alcohol-induced stupor. The man had his arm tightly around her neck, a beer bottle in his hand. A lit cigarette protruded from his free hand. They spun in a circle in front of Eden and Elizabeth, blocking the sidewalk. With a menacing eye the man looked at Elizabeth, up and down. He smiled at Eden; an upper central incisor was missing giving him a Jack-o'-lantern appearance.

"Trade ya," he said. "This bitch for yours," he said, nodding toward the headlocked blonde.

Eden knew immediately that the fight was on. He knew from experience there would be no talking his way out of the confrontation. The man was drunk, but the look in his eyes and the scars on his face told Eden that it would have happened with or without the influence of alcohol. In the bars of Da Nang he had seen men knife each other with little provocation, often over whores. They referred to their fleshy chattel as bitches and were quick to fight in order to protect their harems.

Eden released his grip on Elizabeth's hand and clutched her above the elbow, guiding her off the curb, into the street.

The man flicked his cigarette at Eden. Missing him, it bounced off Elizabeth's shoulder in an explosion of sparks.

"Hey, I'm talkin' to you, asshole," the man said. Releasing his grip on the drunken woman, he attempted to grab Eden's arm.

There was no broadcasting of Eden's movements, no eye contact, no words or chest beating, only an unexpected blur of bone crushing strikes. A left jab with fingers extended caught the man squarely in the larynx. Eden's right fist struck powerfully in the center of the man's face, shattering his nose. It was over in less than a second. The man sank to his knees; clutching his throat, he gasped and choked in an attempt to breathe. Blood immediately began to gush from his nose. Hot with aggression, Eden caught himself before delivering another blow.

"You bastard!" the woman screamed as she hovered over the gasping man, who was now on his hands and knees. Blood puddled on the sidewalk beneath him; beer chugged from the dropped beer bottle.

Eden took Elizabeth by the arm and briskly escorted her across the street. She said nothing, but the look on her face made his heart sink. He saw in her eyes the realization that the man she had just married possessed the capacity to kill. It had always been there, lingering just beneath the surface, a haunting reminder of Vietnam. He had no idea how many men he had killed. He refused to count. Most were at a distance, targets that had fallen without making eye contact or begging for mercy. Smoke, noise, and incoming rounds had confused the act of killing with that of survival.

Death had been all around him. He was a dispassionate observer of its true meaning, calloused by the carnage of man's inhumanity. Repression of the truth was a full-time job. At night, when his guard was down, he cried in his sleep. But this was real; he was wide awake and it was terrifying to feel the familiar kill or be killed mentality bubble to the surface and spill over him with the heat of battle. Point and pull, it had been that simple. Now he was exposed.

They stopped on the narrow catwalk of the highway bridge, high above the river. Eden clutched the railing tightly and stared at the blackened water below. Neither of them spoke. Neither knew what to say.

"Are you all right?" Elizabeth whispered.

"Beth, I'm sorry. This is not what I had in mind for our wedding night," he said shaking his head.

"You frightened me back there," she said, then paused. "I don't know if you were defending my honor or if it was some male, macho, competitive thing. But you needn't kill someone in order to have me as your wife."

He turned suddenly and stared at her sharply, searching her face for some indication that she knew who he was.

"Eden, you're scaring me again. What is it? What's wrong?"

He continued to stare at her, then mustered a half-smile before turning away. "You once told me that the past makes us who we are, that it shapes the future. Well, sometimes the past just sort of jumps out at you when you least expect it. You don't know what form it's going to take and you may not know what happened until it's over. But boom, there it is in living Technicolor, warts and all. You just saw a wart, a little virus I picked up in 'Nam. The medical term is 'crazy' or, as we used to say, 'fucking nuts.'" He waited for her reaction. There was none. He decided to push it further. "You married a head case, Beth. You would have found out sooner or later, but on your wedding night, wow."

"You keep referring to it as my wedding night. It's our wedding night, Eden. I married you for who you are, warts and all. And quit feeling sorry for yourself," she said, with an edge to her voice. "You're alive. You made it home." She turned away, clasping her upper arms against the cool evening.

Lightning flashed in the distance followed by a low rumble of thunder several seconds later. He put his arm around her and gently pulled her to his side as they both stared toward the water, staring without seeing, talking without speaking.

*****

The Garfield was dark and smelled of old things. The floors creaked loudly, aged protests to every step and movement. They were the only guests. The owner, a surly, middle-aged man with an unseen wife, lived somewhere below the second floor suite. They showered separately in a stall so small that Eden's elbows banged against the sides. Elizabeth called the Gudmunsons to check on Jessica, her voice strangely loud in the cavernous room. All other conversations were whispered, muted by circumstance, physical and emotional. The high, antique bed with walnut head- and footboards screeched with a springy twang as they crawled to the top of the feathery mattress. Once in place, they lay silently, holding their breath for fear of signaling carnal pleasures to the owners below. They held hands without looking at each other.

*****

The storm front moved gently overhead at midnight. In its wake a dense, black sky released a steady rain. Eden sat in one of the two overstuffed chairs in the bay of the turret that formed the outside corner of the room. He watched the rain through the glassy imperfections of the tall windows. Distant lightning illuminated the slow-moving river, its surface agitated by the rain. The sound of water flowing steadily through an unseen downspout was soothing. But he could not sleep.

Elizabeth lay on her side, facing away from him. He hoped she was asleep. His head was so full of thoughts that he could not finish one. Random outbursts from a tormented brain made it difficult for him to swallow the lump in his throat. A lump that only added to the sickness he felt in his stomach. One thing was certain: He had gone too far. His unplanned life had turned a corner when he'd stood in front of Judge Olson the previous afternoon. He could never tell her now. He would never tell her. He had given her the impression that he could hurt or kill without remorse. But there was remorse, more than he could ever explain, and he did feel sorry for himself. Guilt was his wound. A throbbing, festering casualty of a war he hated more now than ever before. He had killed with a sense of emotional detachment; he had been a machine that devoured life. But they had been Viet Cong, legitimate kills in an illegitimate war—all but one.

Lightning flashed, and in the millisecond of illumination it produced he saw him standing beneath a tree at the river's edge. *Rain drenched, he stared upward without expression; their eyes met as they had so many years ago.*

Eden closed his eyes and concentrated on the tinkling sound of water in the downspout. He heard voices, distant gossip within the murmuring of falling water: one-word incriminations, plaintive accusations that whispered *murderer.*

CHAPTER 20

"Surely you wouldn't grudge the poor old man
Some humble way to save his self-respect . . ."
Robert Frost
"The Death of the Hired Man"

1994

THE PULLEYS SQUEAKED AND CLAPPED AGAINST THE flagpole. The layers of silver paint and rust on the pole's surface provided little cushion to the spring-loaded clasps which secured the flag's grommets. Eden had not expected that raising the flag would toll the residents and shopkeepers of Keotonka to the town square. He was tying off the rigging line when he heard the rushed jingle of Roy Ivanson. From the corner of his eye he saw the overweight town marshal attempting to run across the street from Town Hall. Excessive law enforcement paraphernalia bounced and tinkled from his dark brown uniform and danced reflectively in the April sun. An ever-present streak of brown drool glistened at the corner of his mouth from the wad of chewing tobacco he kept tucked in his cheek. Roy reminded Eden of Andy Devine's portrayal of Jingles, Wild Bill Hickok's sidekick in some 1950s television show.

"Eden, what the hell do you think you are doing?" Roy asked. His voice was comically high and always tapered to a whine.

"Good morning, Roy. You ought not to run like that. If you have a heart attack, there isn't anybody in town who'll give you mouth-to-mouth," Eden said. He stood back, shielded his eyes from the sun, and looked upward at his accomplishment. Old Glory waved gently in the morning breeze, billowing and furling at full mast, where Eden believed it was intended to be.

"You bring that flag back down to half-mast right now," Roy ordered. "Flags have been ordered to be flown at half-mast for a full week."

"Who ordered it?" Eden said.

"The president of the United States," Roy said, sounding out each syllable with authority.

"You sure, Roy? Show me the order."

"I don't have any order. I read in the *Des Moines Register* that flags have been ordered to be flown at half-mast."

"You believe everything you read in the paper? Show me the order."

Roy thought for a moment. "Goddamn it, Eden. You lower that flag or we're going to have us some trouble right here."

Eden scanned the small crowd of locals who had gathered on the sidewalks to watch the confrontation. The event would be told and retold for weeks, even months or years, to come.

"Now what kind of trouble would that be, Roy?" Eden asked, turning to face him.

"I'll be forced to arrest your sorry butt and if you resist, I'll have to subdue you." Roy's eyes were bulging with excitement.

Eden could not help smiling at the thought of being subdued by Roy. "Arrest me for what, Roy? What would be the charge? You can't arrest me unless I've broken the law."

That seemed to take the wind from Roy's sails. He scratched his head then straightened his Smokey Bear hat.

"The president of the United States is dead. Out of respect we are going to fly our town's flag at half-mast. Now you run that sumbitch back down the pole. Hear me?" Roy said. He placed his hand on the holster of his gun.

Eden looked at Roy for a long moment, debating in his mind whether to engage Jingles in a philosophical discussion regarding the amount of respect due Richard Nixon. He decided his arguments would be lost on a guy whose deepest thoughts were of cheeseburgers.

"Roy, do you realize how painful it would be to have that nine millimeter shoved up your ass? It would be almost as painful as the embarrassment you would suffer when I tell the folks in town about you liking to wear women's underwear. And what about the time I caught you spanking your monkey while parked across the street from the grade school playground?"

"What the hell are you talking about?" Roy said, turning red, his eyes bulging again.

"Hell, I don't know, Roy. I'm just making stuff up. But I'm a pretty credible guy in this town. Who they gonna believe, me or you? If you want that flag lowered, you'll have to do it yourself." Eden brushed Roy's shoulder as he stepped by him and walked away. "Oh, Roy," he called without stopping. "We'd love to have you stop by the farm for coffee and pie when you're in the neighborhood. Elizabeth asks about you."

* * * * *

"Have you heard from Jessica this week?" Eden asked between mouthfuls of pasta Alfredo. Elizabeth seemed especially quiet at dinner. He knew something was troubling her.

Elizabeth deliberately took her time in responding. She dabbed the corners of her mouth with her napkin then drank from her water glass. "After sixteen years of marriage, I thought I had a pretty good idea of who you were," she said.

"Then I hear that you pulled some crazy stunt in the middle of town and almost got arrested."

"News travels fast around here," Eden said, leaning back in his chair. He knew the meal was over.

"Daddy would roll over in his grave if he knew what you had done."

"You know, I'll bet the elbows of that new suit we buried him in are completely worn through from all the rolling over he has done," Eden said. He bristled at the dead father routine that she was about to deliver. Carl had been dead for seventeen years and with each passing year, he seemed to acquire greater wisdom. Carl's conservative views were now regarded as religious doctrine that demonstrated prognostic wisdom of mythical proportions.

"My father was a respected member of this community—"

"Here we go," Eden said, bracing himself for the argument.

Elizabeth paused. "You're right. We always seem to plow that same furrow when we disagree. As an only child, I was close to my father, and he became the standard to which I compare you. That's not right. I'm sorry."

As a teenager, Jessica had compared Eden to the father she had never known. Spoken or unspoken, Eden felt that he was always being compared and contrasted to men who had never been mortal. Only recently had he begun to accept that he would never measure up to the expectations he and others had of him. He had lived half of his life in the shadow of others. When he occasionally stepped from the shadow into the sunlight, people were quick to remind him of his inferiority.

"Do you want to talk about it?" she said.

"Not really."

"Was it about Nixon? Were you trying to make some kind of statement?" she said softly.

"Maybe. I don't know. I just saw that flag at half-mast and got mad as hell. I had to do something."

"Mad at what?"

"I don't know. Nixon some, society in general, I guess. It makes me angry that as a country we forget so easily. We should be celebrating, not mourning, not showing reverence for the man who lied, cheated, and murdered his way to political ruin. How can we, as a country, forgive that?"

"Murdered?"

"Vietnam," Eden said casually.

"What about Kennedy and Johnson?" she asked. "They presided over the war, too."

"I only know about Nixon."

"What do you know about Nixon? Why do you hate him so much?"

Eden thought for a moment. "Maybe it's not Nixon. Maybe it's the American public. Nixon was a masterful but ruthless politician doing what he had to in order to survive politically. It was the public who tied his hands. Perhaps it was their unrealistic expectations that turned him into the monster he became. The same public that now stands solemnly at his graveside remembering the greatness of their fallen leader. Well, that's bullshit. The two-faced public can hardly wait to get the dirt in the hole and bury the reminder of their guilt." Eden stopped; his knuckles were white from the fists he clenched so tightly. "Don't get me wrong, I'm not making excuses for him. He was weak, treacherous, and insanely self-absorbed. When that hole is filled in, I'd like to be first in line to piss on it."

Elizabeth sat silently looking at him. Seldom had she seen her husband express such anger. But, he had never wavered in his hatred for Richard Nixon. The mere mention of his name would invariably elicit a harsh comment and shift his mood. "And?" she said, inviting him to continue.

"And what?" he said sharply.

"What else?"

"Nothing else. I'm sorry that I get so worked up about the guy. He's dead. I hope he rots in hell. Case closed. Good dinner. Thanks." Eden picked up his plate and glass and disappeared into the kitchen.

Elizabeth heard the kitchen door close. He would go to the barn until his anger subsided. She sat there long after he had left the house.

*****

Eden shoveled a scoop of corn into the hog feeder. The unexpected offering created a stir within the pen, the pigs running, grunting, and squealing as they jockeyed for position at the trough. They kept the hogs only out of respect to Carl's memory. They lost money and time on them. Carl had been fond of saying, "An Iowa farm without hogs is not a farm." Eden knew that corn and soybeans paid the bills; the hogs were an expensive nuisance. Huge hog confinement operations managed to capture the slim profits of pork production while depressing the prices with efficient overproduction. He could not compete.

Jessica had loved to play with the baby pigs when she was growing up. She would dress them up and haul them around in her wagon, chattering nonstop with excitement. He often felt sorry that she had no siblings with whom to interact and was reduced to talking to pigs. Elizabeth believed that the age difference between Jessica and a new baby would have been too great. As an only child, Elizabeth failed to see the advantages of having brothers and sisters. Three years into their marriage, Eden had had a vasectomy.

Twenty years earlier on August 8, 1974, at 8:01 p.m., Eden had run from his apartment, yelling and dancing with excitement as Nixon continued his resignation speech. The next morning, debris from an entire string of Black Cat firecrackers and several empty beer bottles had littered the ground below the flagpole in town square, evidence of his joy. Now, two decades later, the joy had been replaced by relief. Somehow he hoped that Nixon's death would end the nightmares and shatter the vision that played and replayed both day and night. He wanted peace. He wanted to hold Elizabeth in his arms and cry until the tears no longer flowed, to beg forgiveness, to curl into a ball and quietly drift away from the life that tortured him. He wanted another chance, another life, a life without guilt; but, a life that included Elizabeth. She had to be there.

*****

Sleep came slowly for Eden that evening. He listened to Elizabeth's steady breathing beside him. Shadows of cottonwood branches with small, new leaves danced softly against the confusing wallpaper pattern. He refused to dream of Vietnam.

When he finally closed his eyes, the road ahead was straight and flat, the desert a light brown. The long, dark hood of the slope-backed Hudson sedan stretched out before him. The divided windshield was mottled with the dried remains of insects. Elizabeth sat quietly beside him, smiling pleasantly. There was no sound. President Nixon sat in the backseat. He looked comfortable in spite of his dark suit and tie with a stiffly starched white shirt. He, too, smiled pleasantly, occasionally turning his head to look out the side windows. Eden watched him in the rearview mirror. He thought that Nixon looked small slumped in the middle of the huge overstuffed backseat. Somehow he had imagined him as a much larger man. His hair was unnaturally dark and he wore makeup.

In the distance a child herded animals along the side of the road. As they sped toward them, he recognized Jessica, her blonde hair flowing over her shoulders, stick in hand, walking slowly behind a half dozen pigs. Each animal was dressed with some article of clothing, a T-shirt or pair of shorts, a scarf. One pig wore a pink tutu around its midsection. Everyone turned to watch her as the car sped past. No one spoke.

Elizabeth seemed to smile more broadly as she gazed down the road in front of her. Even Nixon appeared to enjoy the delightful contradiction. Far ahead and to the right, a dark speck darted and weaved toward the road. Eden strained to see what it was. Storm clouds rolled toward them from the horizon, purplish black with flame orange at its center. Rain splattered the windshield, large drops that hit with the force of bullets. The wipers smeared the rain across the yellow-brown insect stains, making it difficult to see. Elizabeth's expression had turned to one of concern, but Nixon continued to smile. The dark figure running to intercept them was a man. He crouched as he ran; his dark, wet flight suit was torn and covered with mud.

Expansion joints along the ribbon of concrete beat rhythmically against the tires, a dull *whump, whump, whump* that became the sound of the main rotor. The man reached the edge of the highway as the Hudson hurled by. He reached out with muddy hands in a pleading gesture, fear and last-second recognition in his expression. Elizabeth thrust her hands against the door window, her head twisted sharply as she attempted to track the figure into the receding distance. Nixon smiled broadly.

CHAPTER 21

"Now so soon as early Dawn shone forth, the rosy-fingered,
the dear son of Odysseus gat him up from his bed,
and put on his raiment and cast his sharp sword about
his shoulder . . ."
Homer
The Odyssey

1973

"WARREN AIR FORCE BASE, CHAPLAIN'S OFFICE," THE woman said, answering the phone.

"Yes," Eden said, unsure of himself. "I'm wondering if you might help me."

"I'll try, Sir."

"I'm looking for a friend who's in the Air Force and I don't know who to call to get his address," he said.

"Is your friend here at Warren, Sir?"

"No, I don't think so. I was hoping there was some master registry or something where we could just look up his name and get his home address."

"The United States Air Force is a very large organization, Sir. Do you know what base he is stationed at?"

"No. I last saw him in Vietnam about a year ago."

"This is the Chaplain's Office, Sir. Did someone refer you to this number?"

"No. I just didn't know where to start," Eden said.

"Are you here in Cheyenne?" she asked.

"No, I'm calling long distance." He had to be very careful. He was calling from a pay phone in the basement of the student union in Laramie.

"Well, Sir, if I could get your name and number, I'll find out who you should call and get back with you."

Eden hung up the phone. His hands shook. But he knew what was right and what had to be done. He fumbled in his pocket for more coins.

"Information. What city?"

"Traverse City," he said

"What listing?"

"Robinson. Shelly Robinson." He had no idea if she had gone home to Michigan or had a separate listing.

"Here you go," said the operator, and a pleasant computer generated woman's voice gave him the number.

"*We'll watch you, we'll test you. You fuck up, we'll kill you,*" the SOG Colonel had said. Eden believed him. He nervously placed the receiver in its cradle. They could be tapping her phone, or at a minimum checking her phone records. They knew where he was. Any incoming call with a 307 area code would be a red flag. He had to be the only SOG–cleared grunt from Wyoming. But he had to think of her, too. He had asked her for help once before and she had paid a heavy price for listening. He could fly to Michigan and use up a month of his GI Bill, or call her.

An Army captain stepped from the barber shop and walked toward Eden. Eden froze. He wanted to run, but instead stood next to the pay phone and stared open-mouthed at the crisp officer.

"Good morning," the captain said as he passed by.

"Good morning, Sir," Eden said softly, looking down. He watched as the officer disappeared into the faculty dining room. ROTC, he realized, but his heart still pounded heavily and he had difficulty catching his breath.

"Hello."

"Could I speak to Shelly Robinson, please?"

"This is Shelly."

Her crisp, upper Midwest voice was familiar. "Shelly, this is Eden Cain. I'm sure you don't remember me, but we met about a year ago in Da Nang." He paused, biting his lower lip, waiting for her recognition.

"Yes," she said suspiciously.

"You gave me books." He closed his eyes in embarrassment. She had given thousands of books to hundreds of GIs. "Um, *The French Lieutenant's Woman* and *The Summer of '42*. We talked about them."

"Oh yes, I remember. Sorry. How are you, Eden? I mean, are you okay? You made it home alive, but are you all right?"

"I'm fine, thanks," he said, looking down at the floor and seeing nothing. He was not fine. He had not been fine for a long time. "How are you doing?"

"I'm quite well, thank you. I'm engaged," she added boldly.

"That's great. Congratulations." He knew she had thrown in the engagement announcement, whether it was true or not, to discourage any romantic intentions he might have. "I'm really happy for you," he added, trying not to show any disappointment.

"Thanks."

There was an uncomfortable pause while Eden tried to determine how best to proceed. "Do you really remember me?" he asked suddenly.

"Yes. Absolutely. You're the guy with short hair and an olive drab uniform." She paused, but Eden did not respond. "Just chiding, Eden, of course, I remember you. You were a member of an Army helicopter crew. You're the cowboy from Wyoming." She paused again. "The guy with pretty green eyes and long, dark lashes," she added softly.

Eden blushed slightly. "Right, the cowboy from Wyoming."

"Where are you?" she asked.

"I'm in Wyoming. Laramie. I got accepted to grad school. I'm working on a master's."

"That's great, Eden, congratulations to you, too."

"Thanks, Shelly." He paused for too long, and said, "It's good to hear your voice. It's good to know you made it back in one piece, too."

"Someone who looks like me made it back," she said. "I'm pretty sure I'm not the same person. Know what I mean?"

"Exactly. I keep waiting for the real me to show up." He paused again, then looked up and down the hallway. "While I'm waiting for my return, I thought I would work on a few loose ends. Things I need to do. Things that might make me feel whole again."

"Was talking to me one of those things?" she asked.

"Yes," he said without hesitation. "And I'm feeling better already. Maybe we could sort of stay in touch. Start our own book club or something."

She laughed and said, "I'd like that."

"Shelly, I had two reasons for calling you. Two loose ends. You were the biggest loose end."

"Watch it, buster," she said. "What's the other one?"

"Do you remember me asking you about how to locate an acquaintance of mine? He was in the Air Force and I only remember his last name."

"Yes, I remember. You haven't found him yet?"

"No, not yet."

"I did some checking and then some things happened and I . . . I never had a chance to get back with you. I ended up coming home. I was sick for a while."

Eden did not know what to say. *How do you respond to someone who has been raped?* he wondered. "I'm sorry to hear that. I hope you're okay now."

"I'm getting there. I've got a great job working for a state representative. I think Representative Roberts is going places."

"That's great, Shelly." He paused and then added much too quickly, "Were you able to find out anything about the pilot?" He winced at how it came rushing out.

"I don't remember exactly. I checked with my supervisor at China Beach, but she said that without a serial number or unit it would be impossible to find him. So, I marched right into General Tucker's office at the Da Nang Air Base. He left the Air Force a few months later and Nixon appointed him to some high-level job, something to do with national security. Anyway, it was all very confusing, as I recall. There were lots of Air Force guys running around, but I learned that the Marines used that base as much as the Air Force. Did you know that the Marines did a lot of the bombing over there?"

"Yes, I knew that," he said.

"Anyway, the general told me that the Navy flew mostly off of aircraft carriers out in the Gulf, and the Air Force crews were coming out of Guam with the big planes and Thailand with the smaller ones. Most of it went right over my head. By the time I left, I was really confused and I wasn't sure I had learned anything other than the Air Force was huge and you can't find somebody unless you know their unit or serial number."

"But you had told him the name I was looking for?"

"Yes, I can't remember it now. But at the time, I'm sure I gave it to him correctly. He asked if I was sure that the guy was in the Air Force. They did have an Air Force unit there, you know. It was called the 366th Tactical Fighter Wing. I remember that because I used to take books to them. A day later is when I got real sick and was sent home. I guess I didn't find anything out for you."

"No, you were great. I really appreciate everything you did." She had been raped and beaten within twenty-four hours of mentioning Hallingbye's name to the Commanding General. The flyboy had been in the Air Force for sure. Eden remembered the USAF letters boldly displayed on the tail section of the smoldering Thunderchief wreckage. He also knew that the 366th was mostly made up of F-4 Phantoms; the MIG masters were air-to-air combat planes, more agile than the F-105 Thunderchief bombers. The Thunderchief was probably out of Thailand. But the CG had known something and had made a call, probably to the CG at XXIV Corps. Shelly had paid the price for her innocence.

"I hope you find him," she said, breaking the long silence.

"Thanks. Me, too."

"You will. You found me, didn't you?"

"You were easy. I'm just lucky you weren't married. I mean, I'm lucky you're still using your maiden name; I mean, *your* name because you're not married yet, right? You know what I mean?"

"I think so," she said, with some hesitation.

"Good. I'm glad one of us does."

Eden thanked her and they stumbled over contacting each other in the future before saying goodbye. The operator informed him of his charges and he deposited most of the change from his pocket. He remembered Shelly's radiance in a land of darkness. She had brightened his life and been repaid with savagery. It was possible he had placed her in harm's way again.

Passing the student lounge, Eden stopped when he saw President Nixon on the television. It was a press conference in which Nixon was responding to the "third-rate burglary," what White House spokesman Ron Ziegler had called the raid on the Democratic National Committee's headquarters in Washington. With great conviction, the president stated that he had directed a complete investigation of the incident and there was absolutely no White House involvement. "I can say categorically that this investigation indicates that no one in the White House staff, no one in this Administration, presently employed, was involved in this very bizarre incident," Nixon said. The students seemed disinterested and continued their side conversations. Someone yelled "Screw McGovern!" and a light cheer arose. With set jaw and clenched fists, Eden stared intently at the television.

* * * * *

Fall semester passed quickly. His course load was double that of other grad students in the department. He piggybacked his research on corn variety trials that his major professor was conducting under contract with Monsanto Corporation, looking at herbicide residue carryover into sugar beets. Weekends were spent doing plot work at the Torrington Experiment Station, two hours east of Laramie. Nights were spent in the lab and library. Sleeping only five hours a night, he pushed himself constantly, distracting himself, attempting to erase the memories.

At the start of spring semester a cease-fire agreement was signed. America seemed indifferent and tired. Watergate had distracted the press and the public. Kissinger and Le Duc Tho were poised to receive the 1973 Nobel Peace Prize for their Paris negotiations while the country, overnight, forgot the fifty-six thousand dead Americans and the three hundred thousand who had been wounded. Eden could not forget.

Nixon continued to bomb Cambodia.

*****

In late June, Eden successfully defended his thesis. Technically, it had taken him four semesters to complete a master's degree, but in real time only a year and a half. He had been too busy to apply for jobs, but he was not interested in a career or anything long-term. Graduate school had been a distraction, something to fill the hours. Now he had to move on and give purpose to his life. He knew what was right and what had to be done. Then, perhaps, the nightmares would go away.

*****

"National Personnel Record Center. How may I direct your call?" the woman said.

"I'm looking for someone," Eden said nervously.

"What branch?"

"Air Force."

"Hold on, please."

"Air Force Records," another woman said.

"Hi. I'm trying to find someone I met in Vietnam," he said.

"Name?"

"Hallingbye."

"First name?"

"I don't know," he said

"Social Security Number or Military Identification Number," she said in a monotone.

"I don't know."

"Date of birth?"

"I don't know."

There was a pause this time. "Sir, without the person's SSN or DOB, I can't help you."

Eden sighed. "I'm sorry to have troubled you. Thank you for your time."

"Sir, if you could tell me the person's unit and their date of service in that unit, I could check the unit rosters. The roster will have their full name, date of birth, and service number."

"I last saw him in Laos; it was December, nineteen-seventy-one. I think he was stationed in Thailand."

"I need a unit, sir."

"I don't know his unit," Eden said.

This time, she sighed. "Hold on, sir."

Dixieland jazz played raucously in the background when she placed him on hold.

"Sir?"

"Yes," Eden said anxiously.

"I found the roster for the 8th Tactical Fighter Wing at Ubon, Thailand for nineteen-seventy-one. I have a Captain John J. Hallingbye with a DOB of April nineteen, nineteen-forty-six attached to that unit."

"Does it show a home address?"

"Sir, I'm not allowed to give out that information. My records indicate that Captain Hallingbye is listed as Missing in Action on December twelve, nineteen-seventy-one."

Hearing another human being state that Hallingbye was MIA took Eden's breath away. His heart began to pound; he could not swallow and his hands trembled. Did she know? He wedged his head between the phone and the wall, hoping that people in the hallway had not overheard.

"Sir? Did you hear me?"

Now he knew that flyboy had been listed as missing as opposed to killed in action. So that was how they did it. Rather than admit he was shot down while bombing Laos and assassinated on Nixon's order, they simply listed him as MIA. How many families held on to the belief that their loved ones were still alive, hiding in the jungle or captured as a prisoner of war?

"Sir?"

"Yes, I heard you," he said weakly. "Can you tell me where his next of kin lives?"

"Sir, my records do not contain that information."

"You don't show a home address," he said, an edge to his voice.

"No, sir. My records only show place of birth," she said.

"Can you give me that?" he asked.

"No, sir. You may obtain that information by filing a request under the Freedom of Information Act. I can tell you where to write to receive a copy of the forms if you like."

"How long does that take?"

"Generally about six weeks to act on a request for information."

"Please, I promised him," Eden said softly, embarrassed by having to beg.

"Sir?"

"I promised him that if anything happened I would deliver a message to his family."

"Really, sir, I don't have that information. The Veterans Administration may have the address of next of kin. They will forward a letter for you."

"What I have to tell them can't be put in a letter. It wouldn't be the same."

"I understand, sir," she said, a note of sympathy in her voice. "Sometimes people don't go very far from where they have their families. For instance, sir, if someone was born in

Grand Rapids, Minnesota, chances are they still have family there. You know what I'm saying, sir?"

"Yes, yes ma'am, I do. Thank you. Thank you very much," he said excitedly.

"Good luck, sir."

"Thanks." He hung up and rifled the pages of the directory until he found the U.S. map with area codes.

"Information. What city?"

"Grand Rapids," Eden said.

"For what listing?"

"Hallingbye."

"Full name?"

"I don't remember. How many do you have?"

"I'm showing three: a Gwendolyn, a Phillip, and a Robert."

"Gwendolyn," Eden said quickly, thinking he would start with the first listing.

"Here you go," the young man said. A computerized voice repeated the number twice while Eden wrote it down.

His hands shook as he dialed the number. He felt for the change in his pocket and hoped that he had enough.

"Hello," the elderly woman said.

"Um, hello," he said. "I'm wondering if you might help me find the family of a friend of mine. His name is Captain John J. Hallingbye."

"Who is this?"

"A friend. Do you know him?"

"I'm Joe's grandmother. Who did you say this was?"

So, he went by the name of Joe, Eden thought. It was probably his middle name. He looked at the telephone. "Bell," he said. "My name is Wes Bell. I was in the Air Force with Joe."

There was a pause. "Then you must know that he's not here," she said, her voice quaking as if she had palsy.

"Yes. Yes, ma'am, I know. We were stationed together in Thailand. He told me he was from Grand Rapids."

"Joe was born here, but his parents moved to St. Paul when he was less than a year old."

"Yes, I'm sure he told me that, but for some reason I only remembered Grand Rapids," he said.

"He's a third you know," she said.

"Excuse me?"

"He's John Joseph Hallingbye the third," she said proudly. "He's the last of the namesake. Joe's father, my son, was killed in a boating accident in nineteen-fifty-nine. My husband passed on in nineteen-sixty-seven."

"Is Joe's mother still living?"

"Yes. But I don't hear from her very often. She remarried after Joe graduated high school and now lives in London. She married a man with three teenage sons. Well, I guess they're not teenagers anymore. But she had her hands full for a number of years. She's not well. She started drinking heavily after my son, John Junior, was killed. With Joe listed as missing—well, I can just imagine."

"That's too bad," Eden said. He did not know what to say. The old woman was sharing more with him than he had expected.

"Yes, the family has had more than its share of tragedy. I worry so about Elizabeth, raising that little girl all by herself."

"Elizabeth?"

"Joe's wife. Surely he told you about Elizabeth and his daughter Jessica?"

"Yes, he did, but I had forgotten their names," he said, thinking fast. "Where are they at now?"

"She moved back to Iowa to be with her father. She didn't like California. She calls me often. I guess she still considers me family."

"Where in Iowa?" he asked.

"The southeast, near a little town called Keotonka. I attended their wedding. Joe's mother was ill and couldn't come. That caused a bit of a stir. Some thought it was because of the Catholic wedding. Joe's family are all Lutherans, you know."

"Yes, I remember him mentioning that. Would you happen to have a telephone number for Elizabeth?"

"I do. Let's see, where did I put that?"

Eden could hear the rustling of papers as the old woman searched for the number.

"I'm afraid I've misplaced it, and I know you are calling long distance. You could call information. She lives with her father, Carl. Carl Peterson. She never took Joe's name, you know. She still goes by Elizabeth Peterson. She's a lovely girl. I guess I just don't understand some of the ideas of the younger generation."

"Mrs. Hallingbye, you've been very helpful. Thank you very much," Eden said, now eager to hang up.

"You're very welcome, Mr. Bell. Thank you for calling."

*****

The cool predawn air rushed through the open window of the Willys, tousling Eden's hair. He could smell the lushness of the river bottom country in the damp air near Ogallala, Nebraska. New tires, an oil change, and everything he owned piled in the back of the wagon gave him some sense of security as he piloted eastward toward the unknown. He drove in silence. An AM radio on a Sunday morning in the heartland gave him few listening options. Letting Jesus into his life and begging for forgiveness would not end the nightmares or soften the memories.

A bug splattered against the windshield and he saw a bullet hole through the cockpit window, John Clay's head slumped against the Huey's door. Just beyond the headlights, dark figures scurried into the bar ditch. At a truck stop restaurant near North Platte he saw Brad Holcomb sitting alone in a corner booth, staring blankly at the untouched hamburger and fries in front of him. Blood slowly radiated from the holes in his white T-shirt. Eden's hands shook uncontrollably. He dropped the change the cashier handed him and coins rolled from the counter to the floor. Looking down with embarrassment, he walked quickly from the store without gathering the lost money.

*****

He left the highway to relieve himself just before Grand Island. The pink dawn had given way to a gray, cloudy day that threatened rain. Cottonwood trees lined the dirt road that circled a small pond, the remnants of interstate construction. Their leaves danced noisily as the storm's front swept down the Platte drainage. Blowing dust caused him to squint and shield his eyes as he walked back to the Jeep. The runner appeared from the squall, breaking into the open from the restless trees. His movements appeared exaggerated as he raced in slow motion toward Eden. The trees bent heavily in the downwash of wind. Dirt and debris swirled about him, but the runner did not shield his frightened eyes. His eyes were windows to an unforgiving soul that pierced the distance between them, eyes that begged to be saved.

CHAPTER 22

"I do not grieve as I might have done,
for I have good hope that there is yet
something remaining for the dead . . ."
Plato
Phaedo

1977

THE DRY LEAVES WERE DEEP AND MADE A SWISHING sound as Eden and Jessica shuffled through them on their way to the house. Her cheeks were blushed from the crisp fall air and the exertion of carrying a pumpkin she could barely see over. With her Halloween Jack-o'-lantern proudly displayed in her arms she burst into the kitchen yelling, "Mommy, Mommy, look!"

Elizabeth sat crying at the table. Wiping tears from her eyes, she mustered a half-smile. "It's beautiful, sweetie, the best one ever."

Before removing his coat and hat, Eden quickly pulled a pad of paper from a drawer along with a marker. "Jessica, leave the pumpkin here and take the paper to your room and draw the face you want to carve on it later. Scary or happy, you decide, okay?"

He filled the teakettle and placed it on the stove, removed his coat and hat, and hung them in the hallway.

"Do you want to talk about it?" he asked, sliding a chair from the table.

Elizabeth sat staring at the table, head down, her hands shielding her eyes from the hair that hung over her face. "Sorry," she said, sitting up and brushing her hair back. "This has been quite a year. I guess I'm just feeling sorry for myself."

Eden did not respond.

"I just get depressed once in a while. I don't feel I have any control over my life. Six years of helplessness. They've seen to that."

"Who?"

"The government."

"What do you mean?"

"The Department of Defense, the Air Force, the State Department, the Pentagon, the Social Security Administration, even the president, you name it. They all have a different story, but they all have the same ending. There are so many stories, so many rumors. I don't know what or who to believe."

"What's the ending?" Eden said softly.

"That he's dead," she said, looking at him. "The official term is KIA/BNR, Killed In Action, Body Not Recovered. Nixon announced nearly four years ago, March of 'seventy-three, that all the POWs were on their way home. He called it Operation Homecoming."

"I remember," he said, the familiar knot forming in his stomach.

"We couldn't even get a straight answer on how many POWs were released; somewhere between five hundred and six hundred men came home. Almost all of them were pilots. Joe wasn't among them. The released men verified that there had been at least seven hundred sixty-six American captives," she said, pushing her hair behind one ear. "At the time of release there were over twenty-five hundred men listed as missing in action. The president couldn't have cared less. Watergate was starting to unravel and the media had a new issue to focus on."

Eden could not help interrupting. "If you'll remember, Nixon also announced that the last U.S. forces were returning home at that same time. The lying son of a bitch. It took Congress another eight months to get him to stop the bombings in Cambodia. And that was only after they cut off his money and overrode his veto of the War Powers Act. I'll tell you, Beth, his resignation that next year was one of the happiest days of my life. Only a grenade stuffed up his butt would have made me happier." He stopped himself abruptly. Elizabeth stared at him with a look of concern. He could feel the veins in his neck bulging and the sear of anger in his cheeks and ears.

"Take a breath, Eden," she said, her eyes darting across his face, searching for a clue to his anger.

"I'm sorry, the mere mention of that man's name and I . . ."

"I understand," she said.

"No you don't. You'll never understand," he said, still warm with anger.

They both sat silently.

"I had no idea you were this involved," he said, rising and going to the stove.

"I wasn't! And for that I feel guilty. But I wanted resolution, some sense of closure."

"And?" he asked softly, the teacups rattling in his shaking hands.

"The government says he's dead." She turned her head and stared into the distance. "Is it closure? No. Without a body there will never be closure. I looked forward to the day when someone would make a decision and tell me if he was dead or alive." She looked at Eden; tears filled her eyes. "Well, that day came today and I don't feel any better."

Eden said nothing.

"I know that he was shot down in Laos on December twelve, nineteen-seventy-one," she said staring down at the table.

Eden watched her from behind. She pushed her hair behind her ears, but said nothing more. He had secretly followed the events, too. Hundreds of Americans disappeared in Laos and only ten came home in 1973. Nobody knew how many local VC prison camps there might have been. The bulk of the prisoners were held in eleven prisons in North Vietnam. But there was no talk of the POWs in Laos or Cambodia. The Nixon administration saw to that. They did everything they could to divert attention away from the fact they were bombing those countries and losing pilots. Nixon was smug in his out of sight, out of mind explanation to the public. If the MIAs and POWs didn't show up in Operation Homecoming in 1973, then they were dead. Every pilot who went down in Cambodia after that was conveniently ignored. Ford did nothing and Congress tried to sweep the previous ten years under the carpet.

Holding his breath, Eden brought the cups of tea to the table.

"Now," she continued, "Carter wants to establish diplomatic relations with Vietnam. A couple of months ago he said normalization of relations was dependent upon a proper accounting of the twenty-five hundred MIAs. The Vietnamese said okay, but it will cost us billions in war reparations. Carter and the Defense Department pulled the MIA card from the table by declaring everybody dead. No MIAs, no need for reparations, case closed." She sipped her tea.

How simple, how politically expedient, he thought, but decided to say nothing.

"I was notified of the change in status two weeks ago. I've called our Congressional delegation to complain and have yet to talk with anyone but pimply-faced aides who lie through their teeth when they say they'll notify the Senator.

"Get this," she said, looking at him. "One of the little penny-loafered, blue-blazered preppies insinuated that my motivation was financial since the change in status cuts my allowance by more than half."

Her blue eyes glistened with tears of anger. Eden followed the outline of her perfect mouth, concentrating on the fleshy segments of her lips in an attempt to mitigate the heaviness descending upon him.

"Now we're hearing reports of POW sightings in Russian camps. I don't know what or who to believe. The past six years have been one day of not knowing followed by another. The message from Washington seems to be that it's over and I should move on with my life." She cradled her teacup with both hands.

"There are lots of details to attend to. None of them are easy. His mother wanted a funeral, military color guard, sobbing widow dressed in black, taps, the whole shebang. Grandmother Gwendolyn wanted a gravestone in the family plot in Grand Rapids. But he's got a family right here in Keotonka, a wife and a daughter. Maybe he should be buried here, at least in memory. I didn't argue with them and for that I feel guilty." Her eyes filled with tears, again.

Eden wanted to comfort her, but the words would not come. Instead, he stared into his tea as his stomach churned.

"I don't know what to do. Do I call an attorney? Do I call Father Rasmusson? But what do I say? 'I need a divorce'? 'I need my marriage annulled'? And what do I say when they ask me about the guy I've been sleeping with for the past two years? 'Oh, that's the hired man. I pay him with sexual favors because no one will give me an operating loan. As soon as I sell some hogs and grain, I can stop loving him.'"

"Beth," he started and stopped. "I—" he stopped again. This was not about him. It was about her. But her pain was his pain, too. The same six years of pain and guilt festered within him and threatened to force its way to the surface. It was there just behind his lips, pressuring to escape in an explosion of disclosure. He could end his torment. He would be able to take a full breath again. He knew what was right, what had to be done. But he was too far gone. He loved her too much now to lose her. She needed him to hold her, to wipe away her sadness and guilt for loving him, the same guilt that enveloped him for loving her. It had gone too far. He'd never meant for any of this to happen. There was no plan.

"I think . . . "

Elizabeth had seen the same look in his eyes the day after her father's funeral. A man without choice, cornered, a man about to run.

"Eden, you needn't respond. I just wanted to talk about it and I needed someone," she paused. "No, I needed you to listen. That's all. There is no answer. I know you're going to tell me to take it one day at a time, be patient, and everything will work out. Good advice. Thanks. That's why I love you." She flashed a toothy grin at him, reached across the table, and took his hand.

Eden studied her face. He could see in her eyes that she did not want to hear the things she feared. She was protecting both of them, him from himself and herself from the unknown. The fear in his eyes disappeared. He smiled back at her.

"That's why I love you," he said.

*****

The nightmare forced him from bed at 4:15 a.m. He made coffee, put his coat on over his bathrobe, and retreated to the back step outside the kitchen. The night air was cold. He could see his breath above the steam from the coffee cup. The red, blinking light of an airplane passed slowly between the stars.

He could breathe again. Not as deep as he would like, but with the comfort of resolution. Of knowing what was right. He would never tell her.

CHAPTER 23

"'Dying,' he said to me, 'is a very dull, dreary affair.' Suddenly he smiled, 'And my advice to you is to have nothing whatever to do with it,' he added."
Sommerset Maugham
As recorded by Robin Maugham

6:00 a.m.

THE TOP HALF OF THE BARN DOOR SHONE BRIGHTLY. The line drawn across the barn by the rising sun was level with the world. It was time.

Turning from the window, Eden looked around the room but saw nothing. A framed newspaper picture of Jessica, yellowing with age, caught his attention. She had been named valedictorian of her graduating high school class. He walked to the picture, touched the glass, and read the caption. It had all been very confusing for her. If ever a child deserved an identity crisis, it was Jessica. "Jessica Hallingbye, daughter of Elizabeth Peterson and Eden Cain, has been selected . . . ," Eden had adopted her the same year he and Elizabeth were married. It was the right thing to do. Keeping her name was never debated. It, too, was the right thing to do, but it served as a daily reminder to Eden of his surrogate role.

It had been confusing for Elizabeth as well. Hope followed by disappointment, then confusion, with twenty-five years of marriage thrown on top as overburden. She had survived. She had helped him survive, too.

He again looked down at the newspaper he had placed on the kitchen table. "Grand Jury Hears Claims of Tucker Involvement. SOG Members to Testify." Tucker had violated the most basic principle of personal and military honor by willingly leaving a fellow serviceman behind. Leaving them behind was one thing, but he had gone well beyond that. He had then falsified records to cover his and Nixon's crimes.

The emotional toll was high on the thousands of POW/MIA families who were asked again to accept the probability of death. The probability of life was their strength, their solace.

The front page article gave the highlights of the events leading to the seating of the Grand Jury. A Senate Select Committee had determined that when Tucker headed the National Security Administration, he had falsified the location of loss data for American casualties in Cambodia and Laos. When a retired Air Force analyst had stepped forward with detailed personal files concerning losses of downed aircraft and pilots, the NSA had conveniently lost all traces of the documents. Eden had not been surprised.

The news article alleged that when Tucker had become Secretary of Defense, he had interfered with and undermined the legal process for settling status determinations of POWs and MIAs by declaring them as Killed in Action, Bodies Not Recovered. Carter had taken the path of least resistance by carrying out the previous administration's policy. The POW/MIA organizations had reacted loudly. Carter's people had had them investigated and attempted to discredit them with accusations of fraudulent solicitations and violations of disclosure laws.

But Tucker and everyone after him had underestimated the POW/MIA organizations' determination. They waited for the right time and kept pushing for declassification. Teary-eyed widows and young professionals who had never known their fathers made great thirty second sound bites on the five o'clock news. It was out of control. Self-promoting politicians and a blood-crazed media facilitated each other. The public yawned with the acceptance of yet another political scandal. Little people like himself would be exploited and discarded. The media and politicians never had regrets. But he did.

He never believed people who, at the end of their lives, said they had no regrets. Life was filled with regrets. Lying about them at the end was consistent with their fictitious view of themselves. He'd accepted his cowardice long ago. He, too, would be consistent. There were no options. He had replayed every scenario a dozen times since receiving the letter. Elizabeth would figure it out whether he lied to Congress or not.

One more look around the room. He had made himself a place here, a storybook home built upon the lightness of untrue words; words that masked his deceptive heart, a heart in constant fear of exposure. His had been a life of cat and mouse games that teased around the edges of truth. If only he had been truthful in the beginning. But the beginning would have been the end. There would have been no understanding and, therefore, no life from which he had to escape. Regrets, he had lots of them. He swallowed hard. *Get on with it,* he said to himself.

The revolver was heavy, stuffed into the front pocket of his jeans; its cold steel chilled his skin. Rodney crowed again, a pitiful attempt at heralding a new dawn. He removed the telephone receiver from its cradle on the kitchen wall. He dialed 911. Holding the phone between his head and shoulder, he glassed the Feds at the end of the driveway. They watched.

"All circuits are busy. Please hang up and try your call again later," the recorded voice said without emotion. Eden held the receiver away from him and stared at it in disbelief. How could 911 be busy? Why not a simple busy signal? He hung up the phone and nervously looked at his watch. He dialed the local prefix and four random numbers. "All circuits are busy. Please hang up . . ." He hung up.

"Sons of bitches," he whispered, again glassing the Mazda. Turning, he startled at the sight of Elizabeth standing in the doorway to the kitchen. "Jesus, Beth," he started to complain, and caught himself.

Still barefoot, she had pulled on a pair of his pajamas. Ill-fitting, they made her appear small; her uncombed hair, backlit through the doorway, shone with silvery-blonde radiance as it spilled over her shoulders. She held the letter in her hand.

"I had a dream once," she said, looking down at the floor. "It was a long time ago. Jessica was little. I've never forgotten it. It was one of those silly dreams that made no sense. But it stayed with me. You know the kind?"

Eden did not respond. He stood, frozen with fear. He listened.

"We were eating, sitting around the dining room table. Dad was there, too; it must have been some holiday, before we were married. The doorbell rang and I answered it. It was Joe. When I brought him in and said, 'Look everybody. Look who's here,' he looked at you, nodded, and said, 'Eden,' matter-of-factly. You, too, nodded your recognition and said, 'Joe.' You knew each other. There was no awkward moment where lover meets husband, or vice versa."

She looked at Eden, her brow slightly furrowed. "It was as if you were expecting each other," she said, almost accusingly. "The atmosphere was cordial. A bit strained, perhaps, but cordial. When Joe said hi to Jessica, she hissed at him with her mad cat imitation. I don't remember much else, except the ending. You and Joe were talking softly, too softly to be understood, as you walked together down the driveway. When you came back, you were alone. When I asked you where Joe was you looked at me with that puzzled look of yours and said, 'Joe who?'"

"Beth," he started.

"The point is, Eden," she interrupted, "I've known for a very long time that you didn't come to Keotonka by chance. I've known from the first day you arrived. Les from the Texaco station told me that you had asked about me by name. Small town, Eden; I've known. I've always known that you were here on a mission."

"There was never a mission, Beth. There was no plan."

"I never wanted to know why or what. I guess I was too scared," she said. "You tried to tell me, lots of times, early on. But I wouldn't listen. I still don't want to know." She held the letter in front of her and said, "I don't know what this is about. I can guess. I've been following the news. I don't care what it's about. Nothing will change the fact that I love you. I've always loved you and I'll continue to love you for the rest of my life."

"There was no plan," Eden interrupted. "Don't you understand? My life with you was an accident. I never meant for any of it to happen. You're right, it was no accident that I came to Keotonka. But I swear to you that the last quarter century was unplanned."

"A mistake?"

"No," he shot back. "Just happenchance; life just unfolded a day at a time. The mistake I made was not telling you. That's my big regret. And God knows I tried to tell you, Beth. But the stakes got too high. I was afraid of losing you. But there was no plan, not a conscious one, at least. I had no idea what I would do when I got here. But then a miracle occurred. When I was close to you, when you held me in your arms, nothing else mattered. The memory that I've never been able to erase would disappear as long as I was touching you."

"I give you relief," she said, her eyes filled with tears. "But do you love me?"

"If you only knew how much. I wish that I could tell you, put it in words that you could understand. That's why this hurts so much," he said, pointing to the letter she held at her side. "I didn't want you to find out this way."

Elizabeth stared at the letter. Tears ran down her cheeks when she looked up at him. "Did you know him?"

"No."

"Is he dead?"

"Yes."

He waited for the next question, the one that would end his torment. But it did not come. She did not want to know, but she knew. He could see it in her eyes. She had always known. Like him, she was afraid of the disclosure.

"Why did you come here?" she asked.

"I don't know. I truly don't. I used to ask myself that question a lot. At the time, I thought it was the right thing to do, that something had to be done. But I never knew what. In the back of my mind, I probably wanted to give us both closure. You needed resolution so you could get on with your life. I needed forgiveness in order to end the nightmares. I didn't plan to love you. When I saw you and Jessica dancing at the restaurant that day, something happened. If there was a plan, it changed at that moment. I fell in love with you, Beth. I didn't want to hurt you. Or, maybe I didn't want to hurt myself. I don't know. I just know that I needed to be close to you. I still do."

"Who else knew about Joe?"

"Just a handful of people, including Nixon."

"Nixon?"

"He ordered it."

"Is that why you've hated him so much?"

"Yes. He made me part of it. But, don't you understand, he robbed more than Joe of his life? He robbed you and Jessica of your life and destroyed mine in the process."

"Your life has been destroyed," she said. Her eyes squinted, revealing the crow's feet at their corners.

"No, I don't mean it that way. My life with you and Jessica has been wonderful, storybook. But lurking just under the surface are thirty-three years of guilt. Thirty-three years of nightmares. Thirty-three years of deception. I didn't have the guts to tell you, and I couldn't bear to face you after you found out by watching the five o'clock news."

Elizabeth stared intently at him, her eyes searching his. "What were you going to do?"

"I—I don't know," he said surprised by her question. His right hand moved to cover his pocket.

Her eyes moved to the revolver's grip protruding from Eden's pocket, then back to his eyes. "Take a breath, Eden. I lost my first husband. I'll be damned if I'll lose my second." Tears flowed freely down her cheeks and her bottom lip trembled.

He took her into his arms and held her tightly. She returned the embrace and found his lips. Tears, too, streaked the morning beard stubble of his cheeks. Tears of relief, tears of compassion. It was over. She knew. She forgave him. She had always forgiven him.

"I'm sorry, Beth—"

She hushed him softly. "I'm sorry, too. Thirty-three years is a long time. I should have listened. I was scared. There are things I don't want to know, things that would have stood between us. Let's not talk about it. I don't want to know who or why. Let's talk about the next thirty years and how wonderful they're going to be, growing old together, getting wrinkly together, dying together. Promise me you'll never leave me, Eden."

"I promise," he whispered, and pulled her even more tightly against him. "I should have told you. I should have told you."

"I should have listened."

"But there were no guarantees," he said, pulling back suddenly. "You would have reacted differently in the beginning. Time heals."

"Perhaps. I don't know for sure. I do know that I was head over heels in love with you from the start. You've been a wonderful husband and father. Nothing can change that. My love for you grows stronger every day, Eden Cain. Wishing for something different in the past only makes you sad."

At that moment she was more beautiful to him than at any time he could remember. He drew her tightly against him, holding her head against his chest, embarrassed by his tears.

"We'll get through this," she whispered. "Together," she added. "And what's with the binoculars?"

He still held the binoculars in his left hand; they pressed against her back. "The Feds, they're sitting at the end of the driveway watching the house. I think they just want to intimidate me, to remind me of my oath of silence. Maybe they want to kill me. But not without a fight," he said, patting the handle of the revolver. He could see in her eyes that she was not fooled by his reference to self-defense as justification for the revolver.

Taking the binoculars from him, Elizabeth stepped to the window for a look. "Are you sure? It's a funny-looking car. Don't they all drive black sedans?"

"Mazda," Eden said. "I'm sure it's a rental."

"Who are they?"

"I haven't a clue. They could be anybody, the FBI, CIA, NSA, AFT, DOD. Who knows, maybe DOA, the Army themselves. I'm sure they're all nervous about the hearings. Probably all of them are implicated. Tucker is a murderer who wants the presidency more than anything. They could be his boys. Listen to me. I'm totally paranoid. It could be the Department of Justice, scared that I might skip out without testifying. If I had to guess, I'd say the FBI. They got the job, but don't know why or even what the issue is. They're just the lackey here."

"Is there someone we should call? What about Harold Gustaveson? He's been the family attorney forever."

Eden shook his head. "Harold doesn't know what day of the week it is. They would eat him for breakfast in D.C."

"But you're going to need an attorney?"

"I don't know. Only if I tell the truth, I guess. Then they'll either discredit me or hang me out to dry. It's a lose-lose proposition for me. Senator Roberts only wants to ensure that Tucker is hanged by the media and that the credibility of the Republicans is undermined. He just wants to plant a seed with the public. This is all puppet theater. They've convened a grand jury for something the majority of the public could care less about. Something that took place before most of them were born. It's about politics. If Roberts goes too far and exposes too much of the Executive Branch, they'll turn on him. It'll cost him the presidency."

"Then let's leave, go some place until this is over," she said.

"I would be in contempt of Congress. They would issue a warrant for my arrest. We have a crop to pick in a few weeks. We have those stupid hogs out there that need to be fed and shipped. We have a loan to pay off. We just can't run away. Where would we go?" He sounded stupid and he knew it.

Earlier he had not cared for the crop, the hogs, or the loan. He had been on the verge of running away, permanently.

"How did you get this?" she asked, holding up the letter.

"Some guy claiming to be a U.S. Marshal that Fat Roy brought out here two days ago. You were in town."

"But what do they want? They just can't sit there all day watching us. This is America. They have no right."

"Maybe we should call Jessica. She could organize a protest," he said, scratching the back of his head.

"We need to call somebody."

"They've done something to the phone. You get a message saying all the circuits are busy."

Elizabeth picked up the phone and dialed.

"Who are you calling?"

"Mary Margaret."

Mary Margaret Lucritz had been her best friend since grade school and lived only four miles downriver from them.

She looked at the receiver then at Eden before hanging up. "Could be a coincidence."

"Unlikely," he said.

"What are we going to do?"

"Nothing right now, business as usual until we can figure this out."

Elizabeth went to the mud porch and slipped on a pair of rubber irrigation boots and a Carhart jacket over the pajamas.

"Where you going?"

"I'm going to jump in the car and run down the driveway and invite them to breakfast."

"Breakfast?"

"I'm sure they're hungry. They've probably been there most of the night."

"That's Iowan of you, Beth, but probably not a good idea. We don't know who these guys are. They could be dangerous."

"Well, if they were dangerous don't you think they would have already been dangerous? I doubt if they'll accept the invitation. I just want them to know that we're not intimidated. And yes, it's an Iowa custom to feed people parked at the end of your driveway."

"Beth—"

"Take a breath, Eden. Put on the coffee. I'll be right back." She flashed her broad, toothy smile and her eyes sparkled irresistibly.

He knew the decision was made and there would be no changing her mind. "Take my pickup. It's blocking your car. The keys are in it. Be careful, you're in my pajamas."

She kissed him softly on the lips. "We'll get through this, just like we've gotten through every other crisis in our lives. We might as well have a little fun in the process." She blinked her assurance, smiled tightly, and stepped out the back door.

Eden watched her cross the barnyard and disappear into the barn. There was a spring in her step despite the awkward boots.

The cap to the diesel tank dangling at the end of its chain, again, caught his attention; something so minor, but askew within his familiar world, flashed in the morning sun. The realization of danger descended upon him with a suffocating coldness. His arms felt limp and his legs tingled with sleepy numbness. For a moment he could not inhale. He remembered Ernie's second string replacement, his Coop cap pulled tightly down on his forehead, filling the tank the day before. It was the same man sitting behind the steering wheel of the car parked at the end of the driveway.

"Oh, God, no. Please, God, no," he said, staggering back from the kitchen sink. He nearly tore the screen door from its hinges as he burst into the yard screaming. "Beth, Beth!" he yelled, a mixture of fear and pleading in his voice.

His legs belonged to someone else, rubbery pistons pounding slowly below him. The world became silent except for his own labored breathing. He saw everything so clearly, so sluggishly. Even his voice sounded distant and garbled as time slowed in order that he see each detail.

The explosion forced all the air from his lungs before knocking him to the ground. There was no noise, only tremendous pressure against his eardrums. From the exploding doorway of the barn, an orange, rolling ball of fire unfurled a long, hot tongue toward him. The heat embraced him; his hands and face felt the sear of the orange monster's breath. There was no oxygen left to breathe. Burning debris floated above him and slowly rained down across the barnyard. The door to his pickup truck landed with a dull thud a few feet in front of him. The barn seemed to inhale, drawing an orange breath back inside, then exhaling a black plume skyward. Burning straw rained down, flaming curlicues that twisted fancifully through the air. A smoldering irrigation boot lay between him and the jagged face of the barn. He stared at it as dust and debris settled around him. Nothing else in the universe existed. But his mind would not comprehend. He could hear a high-pitched ringing in his ears and knew that he was alive. There was heaviness behind his eyes and the dull, listless feeling of being awakened from a deep sleep was confusing. Time and space were independent of each other. His numbed perception gave way slowly, tingling as reality gained a foothold. The pieces came together with the horrifying, unacceptable conclusion: Elizabeth, the love of his life, was dead, killed in his stead. Killed by the same people who had killed her husbands; one outright and literally, the other slowly and figuratively.

Eden came to his hands and knees, head down. The heaviness of reality threatened to force him back, face first into the debris of his life. He shook his head defiantly and settled back on his haunches. He raised a tearstained face to the sky and screamed her name. His voice was lost in the inferno that now raged in his ears; the orange monster roared gluttonously. The high-pitched squeals of frightened hogs were muted by the turbulent transformation of material things to smoke and ash.

A reflective glint flashed to his right. Turning, he saw the Mazda circle around and pull out onto the county road, mission accomplished. Rage quickly mixed with sorrow as he watched the car disappear behind the cornfield. He knew what was right and what had to be done.

The huge John Deere four-wheel drive tractor with dual wheels, front and back, was parked outside the machine shop. Eden ran to it and climbed the ladder with the determination of a pilot scrambling to the offensive. With a puff of black diesel fumes, the tractor came powerfully to life. He raised the blade attached to the front as the giant wheels began to turn. He could see the dust plume above the corn as the Mazda sped east. The tractor rolled smoothly through the fence and headed diagonally across the field toward the river. Eden never looked back at his flattened wake in the sea of corn that stretched behind him. He deftly worked the transmission and throttle, determined to reach the bridge before the Mazda did. The four wheel ruts were ruler-straight across the cornfield between the farmstead and the river bridge. The perimeter fence gave way silently as Eden downshifted for the steep embankment leading up to the road at the foot of the bridge. The tractor's front wheels left the ground briefly, then crashed thunderously in a cloud of gravel dust as Eden skidded to a halt in front of the bridge. The giant tractor spanned the entire width of the road, forcing the Mazda to slide to a stop a few feet from the yellow-rimmed wheels.

The surprise was evident upon the faces of the two men inside the car. Eden could read the four letter incriminations on their lips as they dug under their coats for their pistols. But it was too late. Eden had already exited the cab and he stood on the catwalk above them. There was no hesitation, no last-minute questions of right and wrong. The response was still there after all the years: point and pull, copper-jacketed death. Kill or be killed. The revolver barked in his hand and bullet holes appeared in the Mazda's windshield. It felt good. He emptied all five rounds and wished for more. The two men slumped toward each other, head to head, blood filling their shirtfronts. It was too easy, too merciful. He wanted more. His eyes clouded with tears that burned. His body staggered with weakness as his anger gave way to grief. He looked down at the gun and wished for another round, one more bullet to end the nightmare.

The man behind the wheel, the Coop delivery man, straightened his head and looked up at Eden.

Eden negotiated the tractor around the car and placed the huge blade against its rear bumper. The diesel plume turned black as the tractor pushed the car over the embankment toward the river. The familiar cottonwoods that surrounded the fishing hole stood by dispassionately; their silvery leaves flashed in the morning breeze. The car slid under the surface without hesitation; chrome and steel sliced deeply into the river and disappeared into Carl's bottomless pit. An iridescent mixture of blue and green oil rippled at the surface and vanished downstream.

*****

The rearview mirror of the old Willys bounced, distorting the image of the dark cloud of smoke rising on the eastern horizon behind him. Just before Keotonka the volunteer fire department screamed by him, sirens wailing. Eden stared straight ahead as he piloted the vehicle west. Fields of corn undulated endlessly before him. He tried to take a breath, but could not.

CHAPTER 24

"Tears came to his eyes as he remembered her childlike look, and winsome fanciful ways, and shy tremulous grace."
Oscar Wilde
The Picture of Dorian Gray

Night

SOMEONE ONCE SAID THAT YOU CAN NEVER GO HOME again. But he didn't know who. Thomas Wolfe, or maybe it was Dorothy dreaming of Kansas. Regardless, it was true. There was no home. Everything seemed a dream, a dream within a dream. A gauzy tangle of cobwebs somewhere on the top of his head lay thickly over his throbbing temples. He was desperate for it to be a dream. But he couldn't wake from it. He had never died in a dream, he always woke before colliding with eternity. Perhaps that was the answer.

At Decatur he debated taking I-35 north to Ames so he could hold the little blonde girl who was now a woman with children of her own and tell her in person that her mother was dead—killed in his stead, murdered because she had loved an imposter. But he knew they would be watching her, tapping her phone. It was too dangerous. He had failed to protect Elizabeth, but would not give them his daughter. At a convenience store he called Mary Margaret. His tone silenced her questions and compelled her to follow his instructions on how to contact Jessica. He was forced to stop several times to regain his composure. Mary Margaret wept openly, but agreed to the convoluted process designed to avoid having her phone records give away his westward direction. He needed time. He asked her to tell Jessica that he loved her and that he would explain. He had paused so long that Mary Margaret asked if he was still on the line. *Explain what*? he had thought. Explain his cowardice for not facing the only person left in his life who mattered. Explain why he was running away rather than avenging her mother's death. She would never understand the danger. But he would explain, if he could. He would hold her head against his shoulder and stroke her hair as he had when she was a hurt child, the salve of comfort closing the wound. He needed time. When he hung up, his body was weak with remorse. By the time he reached the river below Omaha, sorrow had been replaced by anger.

*****

There was no feeling of security from familiar surroundings as he drove through Laramie. At Lake Marie on top of the Medicine Bow, he pulled over to remember the summer snowball fight that he'd had with Elizabeth and Jessica. The moon was almost full and still low in the east, illuminating a path of rippling water across the lake to the rocky foot of Medicine Bow Peak. That summer had become a reference point in time for each of them. Their lives had occurred in undefined increments either before or after their trip to Wyoming. Life had happened the summer before or the year after, taking the place of Carl's death as the marker of time's passage. Why hadn't they come back? Perhaps it had been too perfect. Perhaps time had colored their remembrances and the illusion of the past was threatened by discovery. Or, maybe life just got in the way, hogs and corn and soybeans. The things left behind now seemed flimsy, insignificant. It was better to see the past at night.

*****

The feds would conduct a sham investigation and conclude the explosion was an accident involving stored diesel fuel and commercial fertilizer. There would be little or no media coverage. Local law enforcement would be redirected and misled. Roy would jingle around town, puffed up and important. But the manhunt was theirs. He was a fugitive. *A fugitive from what?* he asked himself. *Justice?* There could be no justice for taking the most sacred thing in the world: Elizabeth.

There would be no mention of missing agents. The Grand Jury subpoena would be quietly dismissed and a warrant would not be issued. They would watch Jessica, monitor her calls, and intercept her mail. And, they sure as hell knew where Wyoming was. They were on their way now, he figured, probably would be in Encampment by morning. He would not be hard to find. He was driving a 1953 Willys wagon in the most sparsely populated place in the nation. He shook his head. There was no plan, no mental debate. He had come home. Why? There was nothing left. Even the inheritance was gone. Three generations of love and labor had bought a combine, a pickup, and two years of operating loans. *You can never go home again.*

Eighteen hours earlier he had resolved to kill himself in order to spare Elizabeth the pain of finding out who he really was. But grief had paralyzed him. He could not remember driving across Iowa and Nebraska. He had felt nothing. The Willys' fifteen gallon gas tank forced him to dry his eyes every couple hundred miles, to avert his gaze and not call attention to himself. Funny, he thought, how random his visions had been: shifting fragments in a kaleidoscope, each fragment a different picture of Elizabeth with a different background from a different time. They were all happy pictures. Toothy smiles and devilish eyes, each fragment attesting to happy times as his psyche compensated for the overwhelming grief that lingered just behind the fragments. Grief that threatened to spill over and flood his mind with pictures of an irrigation boot and body parts, of a crying Elizabeth reaching out to him as the helicopter rose slowly away from her.

Sorrow, again, was already giving way to anger. Anger was his medicine, the antidote for grief. It gave him focus, a purpose. Anger was his rebirth. Tucker would pay. They would all pay. He would kill the sons of bitches who did this to him, who did this to her. But, killing was too merciful, he reasoned. Death didn't have to be literal; it could be a slow, painful, figurative death. Political assignation was a good place to start. He would take from Tucker what he loved most, power. He would shame him in front of the world. He would publicly disembowel him. The fraternal order of power mongers would form a perimeter of protection to keep him out of jail. But his stinking guts would be all over the capitol steps for everyone to see, for everyone to smell. There would be the lingering unpleasant taste of political death on the tips of the media's wagging tongues. The feeding frenzy would rival that of Watergate. They would pluck out Tucker's eyeballs then pick the flesh from his bones.

A pickup truck pulling a stock trailer strained up the steep grade as it passed the turnout next to the lake. Eden felt the tightness in his jaw. It was the first time he had felt anything all day.

*****

Just west of Battle Pass, Eden turned onto an unmarked, rutted four-wheel drive road that snaked northward along the spine of the Sierra Madre. The road had changed little in the nearly forty years since he had hunted elk there. The Willys ground along slowly in compound low, the headlights defining a bouncing tunnel of rock and timber swallowed by the predawn darkness on each side. It was the only road within a five-mile radius of the cabin. It had been easier coming up the valley on horseback from the east. Bridger Peak, a solid wall of granite jutting skyward from timberline, prevented man and beast from cresting the mountain and discovering Eden's secret valley. Copper had lured miners here a century earlier. The remains of their efforts lay scattered on the mountain: rusted metal and lichen-covered boards. So many of their shafts had been vertical as they pecked downward, following the greenish veins. But the one at the end of this road was horizontal and wide at the mouth, big enough to back the Willys into. In time, someone would discover the Jeep. He hoped they wouldn't shoot it full of holes, as they had every other manmade object found in the mountains. He left the keys in the ignition.

So much time had passed, more than a quarter century since he had brought them there. He had built it well and it had withstood time and nature. A fallen tree lay across the remains of the loafing shed, but the cabin was intact. Several inches of pine needles and cones covered the porch and lower portions of the roof. Some of the logs had shrunk, pulling the chinking between them loose, but the fit was still tight. Mice and wood rats had found their way inside, their black offerings covering every surface. But it was as he remembered it.

The dusty score sheet from their last game of dominoes lay undisturbed on the table. Elizabeth, Jessica, and

Eden, their names underlined, each with a descending column of hasty additions that declared the winner. Jessica's eyes had sparkled as she'd shouted the final "out." He had held their image for as long as he could, focusing on one, then on the other. He had been desperate to keep them there, fearing that he would lose them forever if he lost his concentration. Elizabeth had smiled at him, stood and backed slowly away, melding into the darkness beyond the illumination of his memory. He cried, then he slept. There were no dreams, only remembrances.

*****

"Eden?" she said, tipping her head slightly. He would have recognized her, in spite of the years. Her hair was short and gunmetal gray. She had gained a few pounds, but carried it well beneath her wool blazer and skirt. It had been simple: a couple of hitched rides, some lies, a few phone calls, and two days on a bus. Shelly Robinson was easy to find.

"Do you have any luggage?"

Still, he could not speak. He was embarrassed. Unshaven and dirty, he could smell himself.

"Eden, do you have any luggage?" she repeated, this time taking him by the arm.

"No, I have nothing," he said, making eye contact.

"That's my car over there," she said, nodding toward a dark blue Ford Excursion. "Let's take you home and get you cleaned up."

She had never married. Her name was synonymous with that of the Democratic Party in Michigan. She still lived just outside Traverse City, where she raised cherries and ducks on a small acreage. She had remained with John Roberts when he had left the State House of Representatives as freshman

Congressman from Michigan. When he had been elected to the United States Senate, he had promoted her to State Office Director and allowed her to operate out of Traverse City rather than Lansing.

"I was young," she said, setting her delicate china teacup in the saucer. "Impressionable, some would say. He was on his way up and I knew it. He's been running for president since he won his first election in 1972." She paused and stared into her teacup. "His wife tolerated the affair because the children were young."

Eden sipped his tea but said nothing. He wore a pair of sweat pants and a University of Michigan sweatshirt, both of which were too small.

"When he was elected to the Senate, his wife put her foot down. The children were in college then." She looked out the sliding glass door from the kitchen. Domestic mallards waddled across the manicured lawn. "John, if nothing else, is a master politician. He invented quid pro quo. He will get you what you need." She paused. "And if he doesn't, he'll have me to answer to," she said smiling. She reached across the table and covered his hand with hers. "You know I would have helped you even without you telling me that Tucker had me raped and beaten."

"I'm sorry," he said. "I wasn't using that information as a bargaining tool. I—"

"I know you weren't," she interrupted. "That was a very long time ago and strangely, I'm not terribly surprised by it. It's not the same with me; maybe it will be when it sinks in a little. It's different with you, Eden. Your wife is dead. That happened less than a week ago. I can understand your eagerness to expose the bastard."

"When will Roberts get here?" Eden asked, pulling his hand away and trying to change the subject.

"I talked with him while you were napping. I'm sure he'll want to line up private security for you. Everything is very cryptic. He suspects that his calls are monitored. The Secret Service never leaves his side. But, he doesn't trust anyone within the government, especially after what happened to LaFollette."

Eden raised his head. "What happened to LaFollette?"

"I'm sorry, I wanted to tell you earlier, but I didn't want to interrupt. Ernie LaFollette was found dead earlier in the week. They found his body in an alley off of 14th Street. The official cause of death was ruled as a drug overdose."

"Funny," Eden said pensively, "I guess I never knew his first name. We called him Roach Face." He, too, looked toward the ducks who had gathered outside the door, waiting, begging. "Does Roberts know that I'm here?"

"No, but he knows something big is up. We have a bit of a code worked out. When something serious is about to hit the fan and I need to talk with him privately, I tell him we have a potentially huge endorsement in the mill and we need to strategize to pull it off."

"When will he be here?"

"He's leaving Des Moines in the morning."

"Des Moines," Eden said, too loudly. "What's he doing in Iowa?"

"We're just four months from the Iowa caucuses, Eden. He'll be spending much of the fall in Iowa."

"I don't like it," he said, then realized how paranoid he sounded. "Are they watching you? When he gets here, he'll have Secret Service agents with him. They'll check out your office, the house, wherever he goes. How are you going to explain me? They'll ask questions, maybe want to do some kind of background check before they let me meet with him. I don't like it," he repeated.

Shelly smiled then looked down. "Eden, John and I are still lovers. Security knows it. They look the other way. It's not about sex, not at our age. I'm his safe haven. We meet a couple times a month so he can unwind and take refuge. The pressure he's under is immense. He tells me what he's afraid of and I listen. I really listen. He tells me what his dreams are and I listen. John has a vision for this country. He—"

"Shelley, you don't have to tell me any of this."

"Yes I do. I can see it in your eyes. You want to know what I get out of the relationship." She looked squarely at Eden. "I love him. I've loved him for more than thirty years. I've known from the beginning that I can't have him. This is the best I can do. I'm happy, Eden. Do I want to be the First Mistress, the Second Lady? No, but if he needs me, I'll be there for him."

Eden looked at the ducks again. Shelly Robinson lived in a different world and it made him uncomfortable. "I understand love," he said softly without looking at her.

There was an uneasy silence before she spoke. "Eden, do you have any money?"

"Are you hitting me up for a campaign contribution?"

She smiled politely.

"I've got about two hundred bucks left. I grabbed all the cash in the house before leaving, but spent most of it on gas and bus fare. I couldn't risk using the credit card. Not yet, anyway."

"What about your daughter? We can get a message to—"

"No," he said sharply. "It's too dangerous. These are evil people. They'll stop at nothing to get at me. I can't put Jessica and her family in harm's way."

"All right, Eden," she said in the same voice used to calm an upset child.

"I killed two people. I was glad to do it," he said, searching her eyes for a response. "There'll be no protection from that."

"John needs you to testify in front of that Grand Jury on Thursday morning. He'll get you into a witness protection program. They'll get you started again."

"It's the same people, Shelly. Don't you understand? They're not going to protect someone who killed two of their own."

"I'm sure the program is set up to deal with this sort of thing," she said, but there was some hesitation in her voice.

"And get started again? What the hell is a fifty-seven-year-old farmer from Iowa going to start?"

Shelly was silent. She could empathize with Eden. She, too, had thought about what would likely happen if John won the presidency. She would be a political liability. No need for a state director, no need for a mistress. His wife would never allow a D.C. appointment, not even an ambassadorship to a third world country on the other side of the globe. "I'll be fifty-five in November," she said absently. "Funny how you end up," she added softly.

Eden looked at her, his eyes searching for the spunky blonde in her light blue uniform, sitting on the steps of the headquarters building near Da Nang, the French lieutenant's woman.

"Do they monitor your phone, too?"

"What?" she asked, coming back from wherever she had been.

"Your telephone; I called you from the bus station. Do they know I'm here?"

Shelly seemed surprised by the question. "I—I don't know. I guess I hadn't really—" she was interrupted by the buzzer signaling the clothes dryer had stopped. "I would think this would be the last place they would be looking for you."

He could see that she was unsure of herself.

"No one would expect you to approach a leading presidential candidate. That's a pretty bold move, Eden, unpredictable and smart." She stood."You can get your clothes out of the dryer and get dressed while I make us a sandwich." She turned toward him and said, "You have every right to be paranoid. I won't tell you not to worry."

*****

"Bring Roberts—front steps Justice Building—9:00 a.m., Thurs." He had placed the note on the guest bed and quietly left through the downstairs patio door. She was afraid. He saw it in her eyes. Shelly would tell Roberts everything he needed to know and would be safe if she stayed close to him. She would identify him for Roberts on Thursday morning.

*****

Baltimore was as close as he could get with the generosity of truckers. The price had been a couple of greasy meals, secondhand smoke, and nearly nonstop instruction on how to run the country and the evils of corporate America. He had listened.

The dark train ride into D.C. was anonymous; strangers invaded each other's personal space without emotion. Passive eye contact and distance-increasing signals; ambivalence seemed to be an art form. Rain streaked the windows. The yellow lights of civilization stretched endlessly, electric dots pitifully tried to hold back the darkness as they marked the way. Elizabeth boarded the car in Virginia. He was happy to see her, but he remained stoic. She smelled of wet clothing and cigarette smoke. "Take a breath, Eden," she whispered without looking at him. It was still raining when he awoke.

EPILOGUE

"The stale cadaver blocks up the passage—
the burial waits no longer."
Walt Whitman
"Song of the Open Road"
Leaves of Grass

Day

THANK YOU, MATT. Yes, just when we thought the fire season might spare us, a major blaze has erupted here in the Medicine Bow National Forest, southwest of Encampment, Wyoming. News Channel Five was the first to report on this fire earlier in the week. High winds and the remote location have allowed the flames to spread unchecked. The Sierra Madre and Snowy Range were relatively spared this summer, one of the worst seasons for fire in more than a decade. But this has the makings of a major forest fire, with nearly three thousand acres already burned. Fire crews have been dispatched from Colorado, Utah, and Montana. I'm told the terrain is so rugged that fire jumpers have no suitable landing zone. Slurry bombers seem to be the only hope of slowing the spread of this fire until ground crews can reach the site."

"Jennifer, we understand the fire may have started suspiciously and that the FAA has been brought in. What have you heard?"

"That's correct, Matt. In a news briefing this morning, a spokeswoman for the Forest Service stated that when first reported last Monday, the fire had already spread over a large area, inconsistent with a lightning strike. Eyewitnesses report hearing a low-flying aircraft shortly after dawn Monday morning. Standing here with me is one of those witnesses, Mr. James Talbot, a longtime rancher in this area. Mr. Talbot, what exactly did you see?"

"I didn't see anything. I was fixin' fence in that pasture over there when I heard the high-pitched whine of a jet engine comin' towards me. It was flyin' real low, right overhead. There was a loud roar, like nothin' I ever heard before. There was a low-hangin' fog in the valley, so I didn't see a thing. But, he was just above it."

"Then what did you hear?"

"Less than a minute later, I heard what sounded like rollin' thunder or maybe an explosion up on the mountain due west from here. I thought it could of been one of those sonic booms or somethin'. When the fog lifted, I could see the smoke. That's when I called the Sheriff."

"You think the plane crashed?"

"No. After the explosion, I heard the jet in the distance, headed southwest."

"Thank you, Mr. Talbot. Matt, we have just learned that the FAA reported no air traffic in the area on Monday morning, but another witness has reported seeing a suspicious vehicle parked near the trailhead leading into the forest the day before the mystery plane was heard. The vehicle is described as a light-colored Mazda sedan with out-of-state license plates. Anyone with information is urged to call the Carbon County Sheriff's Office.

"So, Matt, the mystery plane and the mystery car remain just that, mysteries. Whatever the cause, it looks like it will be

some time before firefighters can get this blaze under control. With winter quickly approaching in the high country, it may be next summer before we know how this fire started. Reporting live from near Encampment, this is Jennifer Hewlett for News Channel Five; back to you, Matt."

"Thank you, Jen. In national news tonight, the Grand Jury investigating GOP presidential hopeful, Winston Tucker, has adjourned without handing down a single indictment. The suspension follows more than two months of testimony and fact-finding into Tucker's involvement in the alleged assassinations of American servicemen during the Vietnam War, supposedly ordered by former President Nixon; this, after key testimony for the prosecution Thursday by an unidentified, protected witness.

"The chairman of the Republican National Committee said the charges of assassination and cover-up were political sabotage and is accusing the Democrats, specifically Senator John Roberts and the liberal press, of a witch hunt in linking Senator Tucker to Nixon's covert operations in Cambodia and Laos. Outraged by the lack of indictments and claiming political cover-up, POW/MIA groups filed a class action suit against Tucker today, seeking unspecified damages for the families of dozens of missing servicemen from the Vietnam era. Washington insiders believe the damage to Tucker, even without an indictment, is substantial.

"This has the GOP scrambling to implement damage control with the primaries just around the corner. The charismatic Tucker—who has raised more money than any other candidate in history and has maintained a slight lead in the polls over the leading Democratic challenger, John Roberts—is, for the first time, trailing in his bid for the presidency. A special two-hour news presentation, 'Disgrace on the Campaign Trail,' airing tonight at seven, eight central, will investigate the rise and fall of Winston Tucker. Our political analysts will be on hand to discuss who will likely be the leading contender in the scramble for GOP delegates in the upcoming primaries. Recent opinion polls predict, however, unprecedented low voter turnout during the primaries, with 58 percent of Americans believing that our government lies to them on a regular basis. Forty percent of the respondents believe reforms are necessary to ensure disclosure by the Executive Branch and to limit the powers of the presidency.

"When we come back we'll hear how eating red meat and egg yolks may improve your memory. Stay with us."

*****

Tiny droplets of water coursed slowly down the black granite wall, halting, pooling in the carved recesses of a written character, then quickly spilling over, their paths interrupted by the hundreds of letters, by the thousands of names. The early fall rain was cold. Beads of water formed on his eyelashes, rain mixed with tears. The smell of damp grass masked the city odors of concrete and exhaust. He did not turn to see the jogger who padded quietly along the Reflecting Pool and disappeared into the morning fog. Tires on wet pavement hissed as the delivery trucks replenished the city in preparation for another day. Above the fog and white monuments, a huge jet lumbered up the Potomac from Reagan. He would follow soon, but there was no plan.

The letters and names remained fixed against the confusion of rain, rigid adherence to military uniformity. Only the water moved. He traced the letters, gray against black, with the tips of his fingers. Left to right and back again with his knuckles, feeling the sharpness of the edges. Water dripped from his wrist.

He looked down at the tattered wallet photo he had propped against the wall's base. The rain distorted the image, but not the memory, of the smiling blonde woman holding the hand of the little girl. It was all he had to give: reparation for another man's life.

A vaporous cloud rose from his lips when he finally exhaled, disappearing as wispy tentacles into the endless sky. Tiny droplets condensed around the gases of life, rising up, joining with all that had risen before: reunions of the physical, repatriations of the nonphysical, all that once was joined for eternity. He could breathe.

THE END

CPSIA information can be obtained at www.ICGtesting.com
Printed in the USA
LVOW121130030212

266880LV00005B/4/P

9 780983 589426